Charles Clarke

The Flying Scud

A Sporting Novel: Vol. I.

Charles Clarke

The Flying Scud
A Sporting Novel: Vol. I.

ISBN/EAN: 9783337068134

Printed in Europe, USA, Canada, Australia, Japan

Cover: Foto ©Andreas Hilbeck / pixelio.de

More available books at **www.hansebooks.com**

THE FLYING SCUD.

A Sporting Novel.

BY THE AUTHOR

OF

"CHARLIE THORNHILL," "WHICH IS THE WINNER,"
"THE BEAUCLERCS," ETC.

IN TWO VOLUMES.

VOL. I.

LONDON:
RICHARD BENTLEY, NEW BURLINGTON STREET.
1867.
The right of translation is reserved.

CONTENTS OF VOL. I.

THE FLYING SCUD.

INTRODUCTION.

For the last fifty years, by almost imperceptible degrees, a passion for the turf has been developing itself among us. Nothing in the world, especially among the passions, can be regarded as an unmixed good; and, although there are many qualities and characteristics in an honest sportsman which form the basis of English nationality, they are often joined with others which fade into vices, the very reverse of that openness and honesty which was once the boast of our countrymen.

If the turf system of this country ever dies, it will only be by burying itself beneath that load of avarice which is well-nigh stifling its best aspiration. However, while the professional speculators who pull the strings are as indifferent to the pastime, as a Poor Law guardian to the sufferings of innocent pauperism, or a sheriff's officer to the entreaties of his prey, there are many thousands of spectators who still love a thorough-bred horse for himself, and the healthy pleasure he affords them ; who fail to recognise in him at first sight, the instrument of wrong, and the unconscious means of aristocratic swindling.

For this greatness of our countrymen of every class and denomination, Mr. Dion Boucicault has catered. He has provided

one of those dramatic pictures which flatter
our intelligence, by reproducing what we
feel to be true ; and which appeal to our
sympathies at the same time.   It was a bold
experiment, but not more bold than successful ; and it is so successful, because
every individual takes it, as it were, under
his especial protection, and pronounces his
own criticism without regard to any voice
but that of his own intelligence or experience.

   To Mr. Boucicault's kindness and ready
permission I am indebted for the opportunity
of presenting the same features of sporting
life in the pages of a novel.   I believe I see
in his drama the foundation of a story,
whose interest may be heightened by more
close and careful analysis of the separate
characters which he presents to you on the
stage of a theatre, and though it be true

1— 2

that those incidents pass less vividly into
the mind by the ear than by the eye,

"Segnius irritant animos demissa per aurem
Quam quæ sunt oculis subjecta fidelibus,"

there can be no doubt that narration gives
an opportunity of enjoyment, which, if less
vivid or exciting, is more capable of exer-
cising the faculties of comparison and
analysis.

One advantage it certainly possesses, and
it is this: your imagination will have fuller
scope: you can invest each character with
the attributes of your own fancy: you are
no more tied to Mr. Neville's idea of Captain Grindley Goodge, than to Miss Joseph's
personation of Lord Woodbie, and though
it is difficult to believe in a Nat Gosling of
any other type than that very excellent one
afforded by Mr. G. Belmore, you may put
yourself—if you please—into your own

boots and breeches, and ride your own
Derby horse in what tackle, and under what
orders you please.

If any pleasure or advantage is to be expected from the perusal of the following
pages, it will be increased a hundredfold by
having first seen the very excellent drama
from which it is taken.

CHAPTER I.

IT was a mild, heavy night of early spring, in the year 185—, that old Mr. Sykes—the owner of Nobbley Hall and some hundreds of acres round it — lay dying. Whatever pangs the prospect of approaching death may have had for the old man, they were all past now. He bided his time with all outward appearance of patience and resignation. Something mourns for us all. The old housekeeper, who crept stealthily across the room from time to time, to watch her master's breathing, had dropped many a tear for him during the past week; and the handsome black retriever, which lay on the hearth-rug, broke away at intervals to lick the hand which had so often caressed him.

The blinds were all down, and the curtains drawn, and the obscurity of the dark oak furniture of the handsome Elizabethan room was made doubly sombre by the light of the solitary oil lamp, which burnt on a round table at the foot of the bed.

The solemn stillness of the house was broken only by an occasional footfall, and the gentle opening of the door, as an occasional visitor from the servants' apartments came to inquire whether anything was wanted by the occupants of the sick man's chamber.

On one of these occasions the old man

turned, and beckoned feebly with his atten-
uated hand.

During the day he had scarcely spoken,
and had only roused himself to take the
cordials prescribed for him by his medical
attendant, and given him by his housekeeper.

Mrs. Marks saw the movement, and went
towards him.

"Mrs. Marks," said he, feebly, but
raising himself with difficulty on his elbow,
"Mrs. Marks, has any one been here for me?"

"It was only one of the maids, sir, come
to see if you wanted anything before she
went to bed." Then she smoothed his pillow, but he continued:

"Has old Nat been in to-night?" and
this time his voice seemed louder, more like
himself, and a curious brightness might have
been seen in his eyes.

"He came in once, sir, but you were asleep, and we wouldn't wake you."

"And didn't he say something? Where's he gone to?"

"No; he said he'd look in early. He's been gone home a long time. It's nigh upon eleven o'clock."

"And what time is it light in the morning?" inquired the dying man.

"Soon after six, maybe, sir," replied she, somewhat surprised at the returning dawn of intelligence, which she had not seen for some hours before. Indeed, she almost thought he was not so near his last hour as they had been led to expect by Doctor Kershaw.

"Have you wound up my watch, Mrs. Marks?"

"Yes, yes," said the woman, a little put out by the unwonted signs of animation.

"It's all done sir, long ago. Try and sleep a bit, sir."

"No; but you can. I shan't want anything till Nat Gosling comes in the morning; and you mustn't let him go away again without my seeing him. Mind, now, Mrs. Marks, I want to see Nat, and I shan't be happy till I do."

Mrs. Marks would have sent for Nat Gosling, but she thought there were no present signs of death about the old gentleman; and Nat's cottage was the best part of a mile from the house, and who was to go? So, after a time, Mrs. Marks fell fast asleep on an extempore bed; and the poor old man thought on and on, through the night, how long it was in ending.

It is desirable that the reader should know something about old John Sykes, of Nobbley

Hall; and while he and his attendant were alternately dozing and watching, I may occupy the time in giving a brief sketch of the old man's career.

It will be noticed that he was plain John Sykes, of Nobbley Hall. He was not t' Squoire, nor t'ould Squoire, nor Colonel, nor Captain, nor, as a rule, even Mister Sykes. If men of his position have nothing else to hang their names to, there must be a militia regiment in the county, which willingly calls an independent county gentleman Captain, or Major. This was not the case with Mr. Sykes of Nobbley Hall; and though he fought hard all his life for some titular compensation by keeping a large and valuable stud (the straightest road to a Yorkshireman's heart) he made no progress with the poor. Wealthy neighbours accorded him some marks of respect, when they saw him leading the Holderness, or holding his own with the Bramham Moor; they welcomed him when a promising young one for next year's Derby won the Nursery Handicap at York, or the Hopeful at Doncaster; but a circuit of some miles of his own neighbourhood would have nothing but plain John Sykes, which is either the greatest compliment or the greatest impertinence that can befall a landed proprietor.

The reason of it was simple enough. How came John Sykes, at the age of thirty-five or forty, into the Nobbley Hall estate? It was no secret, so we may as well tell you.

John Sykes was not a gentleman. Elastic or indefinite as that peculiar English word has become, John Sykes was a gentleman in no respect; he had neither the birth nor the

feeling of one; and all that could be said
for a grasping avarice was, that it was
governed by legitimate honesty. He began
life as a stable-boy, where he earned a
shilling a week extra by doing some of his
comrades' work, and saved another by denying himself the ordinary gratification of a
stable - boy's appetite. As his wages increased with his age and knowledge, he
saved more; and by the time he was of age,
the columns of the savings bank at Doncaster were pretty familiar with the name
and signature of John Sykes. He was a well-
educated, prudent lad; and, as his father
once observed, would make his way in the
world if his "cursed avarice didn't lead
him into dishonesty."

It was this John Sykes who lay tranquilly
watching for the dawn of day and the
coming of his old servant, his groom and

head stableman, with as much life as he
could muster, and as much anxiety as if he
had a message for him from the world to
come."

CHAPTER II.

THE Nobbley estate had had the good luck
to belong to several generations of real
gentlemen, and Colonel Meredith was the
last of them. They all gambled, swore,
kept open house, borrowed money of the
Jews at the expense of their heirs, and paid
their bills and debts when they could, always
without looking at them, and frequently
without taking a receipt; and Yorkshire is
" no that honest " that it could, or " is that
canny " that it could not, withstand the

temptation of plucking such pigeons. To
this Colonel Meredith the said John Sykes
was recommended as trainer. If he robbed
his master for fifteen years, he took good
care that nobody else should; but the truth
is, he did not rob his master. He picked
up honestly every waif and stray he could
lay his hands upon; and whether it was an
useless but good-looking foxhound puppy
from the kennels, or a piece of old iron,
John Sykes found a market of some kind or
other.

While John the trainer was going up
in the world, the Colonel of Nobbley
Hall, the master, was going as rapidly down
in the world; and, as trainers cannot command success, but only deserve it, Colonel
Meredith's racing establishment got smaller
and smaller, as his gambling became more
reckless, and his losses more frequent. At

last an opportunity presented itself for retrieving his fortunes. A colt by Muley Moloch, trained away from home, was regarded as one of those certainties which are obliged to be backed. It was a certainty to the master, and to the whole establishment at Nobbley, from the old housekeeper, the major-domo, and the ladies' maid, down to the very lowest stable-boy or shoe-black. One only person had consistently declined to risk his savings on what he had always declared to be only a probability, and that was John Sykes.

One week before the race he told his master that he could not win the colt, for that he himself knew a better, an outsider, whose trial was unmistakable, and whom he desired the Colonel to back, adding, " You know, sir, I don't back a horse often, unless I've a fancy for one of our own. I've backed our colt for a trifle, because I shouldn't like to be out of the fun if you win ; but as you've trained him away from home, and I've had nought to do wi' him, I make bold to tell you that I've backed the other, and that I stand to win a heavy stake on Mr. Petre's horse, at thirty to one Now, don't be agin' him, Colonel, for I know it's right."

But the Colonel was against him, and John Sykes, within one week, was worth above thirty thousand pounds.

Three years from this time brought Colonel Meredith to grief. Of course, his old trainer had left him, and had quitted that part of the country. But his money had accumulated. He lent it out at heavy interest to racing men at short dates. He had a share in a manufactory, and worked the abominable truck system, by which

labour is paid in the cheapest market, and
sent to find its food and clothing in the
dearest. He made no bad debts, and everything prospered that he handled. The
property of Nobbley was in the market.
The Colonel was dying abroad without
issue, his nearest of kin being one Tom
Meredith, the son of a late brother, as im-
poverished as himself, and the purchaser
was John Sykes, the self-taught, self-raised
gentleman, scarcely yet approaching the
confines of middle life.

One virtue we should record. He re-
tained a grateful sense of his late master's favours, and, in process of time, he let
one of the best farms on his estate to the
very Tom Meredith who would have been
the Colonel's heir had he possessed anything worth leaving behind him besides
his name.

To return, then, to the sick chamber of the ex-trainer.

" Mrs. Marks," said the invalid, opening his eyes, after a short sleep.

Mrs. Marks went to his bed-side.

" Open the shutters, it must be day."

As she complied with his request, the grey dawn of morning stole lazily into the room, producing a ghastly effect upon the still burning lamp. The air was mild and soft, and the old woman opened the window for a moment, as her patient complained of the closeness of the room. He felt, he said, pretty well, but a little faint—" Free from pain, thank God." Then Mrs. Marks administered his morning draught, and replaced his pillows, and made him as comfortable as she could, for he would have nobody else to nurse him. And again he lay back, calmly and composedly; but all this time he was waiting for Nat Gosling, and that other summons, and he could not tell which would come first.

A different scene was at that moment enacting within a mile of the house. Nobbley Hall was a moderately-sized house, of the Elizabethan style of architecture—red brick, gable ends, oriel windows, and a fine entrance hall and staircase of the blackest oak. The park extended beyond the lawn, which was laid out in handsome terraces for a long distance, till it mingled itself insensibly with the open and moorland country beyond. A part of it had been made, by its previous owners, a private course, and it had been improved and enlarged by John Sykes, whose passion for horses and the sports of the field knew no bounds. He had, as he boasted, bred them, trained them, and run them; but since he had lived at Nobbley Hall he had never backed them.

At the further end of this course, on the morning in question, in the dim uncertain light, were four persons; two of them were on horseback, the others were on foot.

The two on foot were Nat Gosling, the old groom so anxiously expected by his dying master; the other was a fine looking young fellow, called Tom Meredith, to whom I have referred before as a tenant of old John Sykes. More of them anon. Here it is sufficient to say, that he united to his occupation of tenant farmer that of private trainer; and he was intrusted by a few gentlemen who kept a racehorse or steeplechaser in the neighbourhood with the care of them. His landlord gave him the use of the private course for his trials, or the training of anything particularly good. They were deep in conversation, while the boys sat apart on their horses, keeping them gently moving in a small circle.

" We shall know in a minute or two, Tom, whether the first trial was a mistake. I almost fancy it too good to be true."

And Nat Gosling buried his hands deep in the pockets of his drab trousers, and turned over some loose money that was lying there. It was a sharp-featured, intelligent face, with some humour and Yorkshire cunning, but not more of the latter than might be considered provincial.

" I tell you, Nat," said the other, " the Flying Scud gave the old horse a seven-pound beating, at even weights. I've given the young one ten pounds more than the other to carry this morning, and that's form enough to win the Derby, now. If my notion's correct, it'll be a race, and the old one will win by a length."

"You're hard upon him, Muster Tom."

"His legs are like iron; and it's as well to know the truth. There's a difference, Nat, between galloping your horse's heart out trying him, and never finding out what he can do till it's too late to profit by it. I'll take care he isn't scratched, because we're forestalled."

"There ain't no one about, think ye, sir? because there's a precious lot o' rascals in the country," said old Nat, looking suspiciously round.

"They won't learn much from this trial, at all events—it'll be all the other way. Now, boys, come out of the cold behind the trees there, and take off the clothes. Come along quick all the way, and begin racing when you get into the hollow. Come away with the old horse with all your might up the hill, Robert, and see how much you can win by."

The boys got off, slipped off the clothing, gave one look to the girths, and were lifted back into the saddles. They went down gently to the start, and in a minute or two were seen coming along at a slashing pace, but it was scarcely clear enough to distinguish, at that distance, between the two. As they neared the clump of trees by which they were to finish, they became more easily distinguishable. Both horses were being ridden, and, notwithstanding the weight, the young one still held his own.

"The young 'un wins," said old Nat, in a hoarse whisper, with his eyes half out of his head with excitement.

"Not quite," said Tom; "it's the last squeeze of the lemon that will do it. No

three-year old in England that ever was
foaled could win at the weight. But the
Derby is as good as in our pocket," added
he, as the horses rushed by, Flying Scud
struggling gallantly on up to the old one's
girths, and only succumbing at the last few
strides, under the crusher he was carrying.

"He's seven pounds better than one of
the best horses that ever looked through a
bridle, and twice as good as when he won
the Criterion in the autumn"—saying which,
Nat proceeded to assist the boys in their
labours—"and if he could but have gone
for the Two Thousand, he'd have been at
pretty short odds for the Derby—but we
must keep it dark."

In half-an-hour more he was at the bed-
side of his old master, and the two had got
the room to themselves. They were not to
be disturbed.

If the reader imagines that there was any great secret to be divulged, any terrible murder to be expiated, or felony to be paid for, he is much in error. Perhaps a more enthusiastic person may expect a conversation more in accordance with the peculiarities of the case. I am sorry to disappoint him.

John Sykes seemed to have settled everything of that kind to his satisfaction. He only took Nat's hand, and drawing him gently down towards him, whispered—

"Now, Nat, man, how did it go? Is the Flying Scud as good as you thought he would be? Has he won his trial?"

And the old man was himself again for a minute or two after Nat Gosling's appearance by his bedside. His eye assumed a bright intelligence, which it had lacked the last four-and-twenty hours; his cheek had

at least a tinge of blood returning to it, if
not the hues of health ; and his sharp features expanded with a warmth which no
other subject had ever roused in them, even
in earlier days.

"Aye, sir, is he ? hist, master, not so
loud," replied Nat, bending down to whisper, and overburthened with the importance
of the intelligence. "He gave the old 'un
ten pounds for a mile and three-quarters,
and ran up to his girths. It's seven pounds
in hand now, and you'll see——" and here
the old man stopped, for he knew his master
never would see his favourite colt again.
" But you'll want to talk of something else,"
said Nat, as he swallowed a rising tear, and
placed his thin, hard hand upon the trans-
parent fingers of his master. " You'll want
to talk of other things, but I thought you'd
like to hear it."

" And so I do, Nat; so I do. It does me
good; it makes me feel stronger; but I
shan't get up again from here, and I'm glad
that it's Tom's nomination now, though I
didn't think of this when I gave it. I say,
Nat, it's no use to keep those other matters
that you're thinking of, for such a time as
this. They want all one's mind, and all
one's strength; do 'em before you come to
this, and then you'll like to hear of a bit of
sport when you can; aye——" and the old
man raised himself with more energy than
his servant would have thought possible.
" Look here, man, I've done all that long
ago. I've thought of you all, when I was
in health. When your old master—I was
a servant once, you know, myself, Nat—is
dead and gone, you'll see I've forgotten no
one. But you want to talk, Nat Gosling;"
and John Sykes laid his head once more on

the pillow, and his white locks floated round
him.

"Don't 'ee be angry, master," said Nat,
whimpering; " don't ye take it amiss, but
Muster Meredith—he'll feel it most. Have
ye done ought by him? He's no lease; he's
spent his life and his money on the land,
and I doubt your nephew 'll be but a hard
task-master. Poor Tom! He's to be married to Kate some day. If it's not too late,
and ye could help him a bit——ye'll mind
it would all a' been his, if the old Squire
Meredith had been a bit harder wi' some of
us. I'm an old man, and shall soon follow
you, but Tom's got all the world before
him, and if anything wor to happen to
Flying Scud, he'd be a beggar to-morrow.
You owe him a turn, master, for the old
place, and all that's gone from him. Do it,
before it's too late, and——"

John Sykes closed his hand tighter and tighter on that of his old servant, then closed them both upon his breast, his eyes opened once more with a cheerful smile, his head fell back upon his pillow, and he was at rest for ever.

Nat Gosling was rather uncomfortable for some time after John Sykes' death. He did not quite know what to make of that last squeeze. Did it mean that all was right, or did it mean "Good-bye, Nat—mind your own business." He couldn't make it out, and he brushed his hat with his coat sleeve half-a-dozen times a-day, and smoothed down his closely-cropped iron-grey hair, and said to himself—

"Poor Tom! now what will he be doing with this Captain Grindley Goodge. They're no great friends; Tom's a deal too honest for him." For Nat knew very well that a

Derby nomination, even with Flying Scud,
was but a small fortune for a man like Tom,
if it did come off right, and a terribly heavy
blow if it didn't. However, there was
nothing to be done or known till after the
funeral, so he went on with his work, and
said nothing about the last moments of John
Sykes to anybody.

"It was a good trial, anyhow, and it
ought to be a few thousand pounds in his
pocket, to a certainty, if he only works the
oracle right. There's nobody knows it yet
but our two selves, and we shan't split. The
boys don't know nothing about the weights,
and I think they're safe enough."

But it so happened that one other person
had seen the trial, and flattered himself that
he knew all about it, too.

CHAPTER III.

On the morning following that on which the trial of Flying Scud, and the death of old John Sykes took place, we must ask the reader to accompany us to a very handsome suite of apartments in a quiet, old-fashioned street at the back of Langham Place. The situation was one which might have been selected for purposes of literary seclusion, or for that retirement which severity seeks in the midst of sensual excitement. Its object in the present case was a less worthy one, as will be seen.

The rooms—which were on the first-floor
—were, as we have said, very handsome;
large, lofty, well furnished, with an air of
costly comfort about them, and opening
into each other by large folding doors,
which were now closed. The front room
was light, and its three large windows looked
upon the street. The back room was darker,
and a large bow window opened upon some
leads, which were surrounded by lattice-
work, and ivy, with other evergreens. This,
in itself, tended to darken the room, and
give a mysterious solemnity to its appearance. It gave it also a pretty rural aspect,
and this quasi-garden could be used in the
summer as an additional smoking room.
The houses behind receded, so that it left
nothing to be desired on the score of air and
privacy.

The back room alone was tenanted, and

that by one man, who was employed, or about to employ himself, in a singular manner. He looked into the front room, in which were the empty breakfast cup and saucer, plates, teapot, and morning paper. He at once walked to the door which led into that room from the top of the stairs, and locked it. He then performed the same office by the folding doors, and the smaller door which communicated with the back room from the same staircase; he was by this means safe from intrusion, or the possibility of supervision. He drew down the blind of the window which looked on to his modest flower garden, and from the table-drawer of a card table, took two packs of cards. He then divested himself of his morning dressing-gown, which had higher claims for its magnificence than its good taste, and commenced operations.

3—2

He shuffled the cards with that rapidity and neatness which is peculiar to conjurers and croupiers, then cut them several times, moving his hands with great delicacy and deliberation, and always looking at the cut card, which was, I confess, out of all proportion, an honour. He then made several " passes " with the cards, sometimes successfully, but not invariably so. Removing his rings, which seemed to occupy too much of his fingers for a man who did not want them to look at (vanity is the ruin of us all !), he repeated these until he became more and more perfect.

Then he dealt the cards as for écarté, and turning up what seemed to be the eleventh card, at first with much deliberation, and afterwards with greater quickness, produced invariably the bottom card of the pack in its place. It's as well to know that this is

sometimes done, as well as yourself; but the
lesson is given not for imitation. He varied
his performances with corks and balls, and
especially with dice, which formed a very
prominent part of his manipulations, the
object of which was to conceal as many of
these things as possible about his fingers,
showing an open and apparently empty palm.
He was at length satisfied with his per-
formance.

"Devilish good," said he to himself; "I
think that will do."

But he had not quite finished. He drew
the curtains closer, and lighted two wax
candles, which he placed at opposite corners
of the table. He then dealt the cards, as for
whist. Having spread the cards to each hand,
as widely as he well could do, he began scruti-
nizing them closely, at certain distances from
the table, so as to catch the light upon them

at certain angles. Then he turned certain
of them over as he looked, which proved to
be aces, kings, queens, or knaves. He
seemed scarcely satisfied with this, for he
took some of them close to the taper, and
began examining the corners with extreme
care. It was a curious occupation for an Irish
gentleman, at eleven o'clock in the morning.

He was thoroughly engrossed in his occupation, when a gentle knock at the door
startled him. He hastily put on his dressing-gown, dropping the cards and dice into
his pocket, and blowing out the candles.
The knock was repeated, and then he went
to the door.

"Ah! uncle, late again last night," said
the visitant, looking at the table and the
candles. "Here's Mr. Chouser coming up
the street, and, as you told me to let you
know——"

The speaker was a marvel of Irish beauty. Every feature was perfect; and she was tall, and beautifully made, with a manner as graceful and dignified as if she had been a duchess. Her eyes were large and lustrous, and she was admirably dressed, as only Englishwomen dress in the early morning.

"Thanks, Julia; Chouser, did you say? Bedad, it's all right; ye'll tell the page to show him into the front drawing-room, where I'm at breakfast, me child;" and Major Mulligan retired at once, while Julia Latimer, for that was the name of the Milesian beauty, beat a retreat as hastily to her own room on the floor above.

Julia Latimer was Major Mulligan's niece.

"Mr. Chouser, sir," said the page; and

most people know what an Irishman's page
is.   This was no exception to the usual
lodging-house shoe-black and knife-cleaner.
Mr. Chouser, however, walked in with an
easy assurance worthy a groom of the
chambers and a couple of footmen in attend-
ance ; and he and Major Mulligan scarcely
thought it necessary to inquire after each
other, having parted about half-past three
in the morning at the club.   His fingers
were at that moment jingling some of the
sovereigns he had won of young Lightly of
the —nd.

   " Chouser, my boy, you're the very man
I wanted to see.   I've a letter from Yorkshire.   The Criterion colt, Flying Scud, 's
not up to the mark.   He's been well beat
in his trial, and the party won't have him
at any price for the Derby.   I always
said he was an overrated horse from the

beginning. I shouldn't wonder if he went a roarer."

"Is the information good, Mulligan? Those Yorkshire Tykes are rum ones to deal with," said the wary Chouser.

" Good? Is Woodbie's acceptance good for a thousand?" replied the Major, by another interrogation.

" Well, I hope so: so does Mo. Davis, for he's discounted it for us. However, the Derby colt business is yours, and I suppose you know it. If what you say is true, the sooner the commission is out to lay against him the better. If once he goes for the Two Thou. (and it's pretty close), and his pretensions are blown, we shall have to lay thousands to a pony about it. He is at nine to one now, and firm enough at that; at least he was so last night."

" Then be off as fast as you can, Chouser;

and tell Mo. Davis to lay all he can, on the quiet, against the horse, and let us know what he's done by to-night. There's the note ; read it yourself."

Chouser took the paper—read it hastily —concluding, half aloud, in the language of the Yorkshire missive, " ' Hold 'orse won heasy, 'ard 'eld.' Yes, all right—I see. But, I say, Mulligan, Mo. is such a frightful snob."

"So he is, Chouser; but there's more of them where he came from. He is not so bad as he's painted. He's an honest man in the way of per centage by the side of Lawyer Shavecote. Besides, we can't do without him, so we must be civil ;" convinced by which argument Chouser went to Tattersall's in search of Mo. Davis, who was trading there on his own account with some paper that wanted a better name upon it

before he could enable the gentleman to
settle his Northampton account at less than
one hundred and sixty per cent. He called
it forty, but that means forty per cent. for
three months.

About four hours, or more, after the visit
of Chouser, by which time Major Mulligan
had dressed himself somewhat more elabo-
rately, there came a second knock at the
door, and this time it was a certain Captain
Grindley Goodge, who followed the page
into the front room. Captain Goodge was
precisely the sort of person one might
have expected to meet anywhere in company with the Irish major. There was a
dashing, easy assurance about him which
was as national as the full-blown swagger
and assumed tone of honest independence of
Major Mulligan, the roll of whose brogue,
hat, and address were certainly the most

insolent on record. He was proud of them all, but more so of his connection with Castle Mulligan; and it would have been difficult to say whether the Castle derived its importance from the Major, or Major Mulligan his from the Castle. It belonged to a distant relation, who did duty for an uncle or a brother, as might be most useful at the time. On one occasion only had he stood for a father, and then the necessity of the case must plead for the adoption. It's a wise son that knows its own father; and the Major may be excused from labouring under so universal an ignorance.

"I've some news for you, Goodge, me boy. I've sent out a commission to lay the last shilling that — that — we ever will have against the Flying Scud for the Derby."

Captain Goodge smiled, and said :

"What! then you've heard the news already!"

"News, faith! it's no news to me: I said the horse 'ud go a roarer; they most of 'em do now. I suppose it's the atmosphere; but there's the letter."

The Captain took the letter, looking, at the same time, a little astonished. He returned it with a compliment on the orthography, and with a remark that spelling and honesty did not always go together.

"By no means," said the Major, with a broader brogue than usual; "there's more of us gets into mischief by readin' and writin', and why not by spellin', than by the want of 'em. But you don't seem to see the pull we'll get out of it. There's Woodbie, and the Duke, and all the Newmarket party are very sweet on the Scud;

and if Mo. goes to work judiciously, we'll get all we want out of 'em at nine or ten to one; only we mustn't wait till the Two Thousand, or there'll be all the loose fish nibbling at the same worm."

" It don't much signify, Major, what you've done about the horse. Perhaps you're right, perhaps you're wrong. The horse is mine."

Major Mulligan's face lengthened with a stare of sublime astonishment.

" Yours ! what ! Flying Scud ? What ! the old gentleman given him to you ?"

" The old blackguard, who's hardly given me a shilling since I came home from India, is dead, Mulligan ; and the property's mine, and the Scud with it. He promised me once, and he hasn't another near relation in the world."

" Then so much the worse," said the

Major, " for the nomination's void, and he won't start."

" Never mind, we must put that right some other way. What do you think of Nobbley Hall, and about five thousand a year? We'll see if we can't make the Scud useful for some other purposes yet. The Derby's not the only race to be lost. Doesn't your mouth water at the handicaps in prospect? I think we shall be able to do the Admiral yet. I owe him a turn or two, and so do you."

Most dishonest men are in his debt.

" Goodge, I congratulate you." Here he shook hands with the *empressement* of an Irishman. " I suppose the old man's death will be known before long, and the sooner we can stop old Mo. from talking the better. I'll be off now. The death was sudden."

" Very. He was taken with paralysis about a week ago, and died yesterday morning at daybreak. The letter desires me to go down directly, and, as the next of kin, I shall take possession, as far as may be. I shall go down and see the place to-morrow, and if you and Chouser like to go down too, why, so much the better."

Mo. Davis had fully succeeded in effecting his commission, and as plenty of friends came to the rescue of the Criterion winner, there was no great alteration in his price for the present. Then it oozed out that something was wrong. The *Glowworm* sounded the note of alarm. Pholus said the owner was dead. Hotspur, of the *Telegraph*, declared it was the trainer only, and that the animal's position was unaffected by it. *Bell* said both were dead, and Argus, of the *Post*, had it, " From the most reliable authority,"

that nothing was dead but the Scud himself, "who was as good as boiled." The
Sporting Gazette said it was impossible that
the Scud could have broken down; he was
as firm on his pins as an oak table surrounded by legs. The Admiral was be-
sieged with letters and queries. "Where
did the bets go? what became of the nomination? could a man give a nomination away
without his horse, or his horse without the
nomination? what became of the double event
if he could run for the Two Thousand and
not for the Derby, or the reverse?" with
many other knotty points, all hypothetically
based upon nothing: to which the Admiral
(there is but one) replied with his usual
talent and courtesy; and from which we
began to doubt whether the derivation of
the latter word might be "court" instead of
"cour." The public, as usual, *sapiens et*

rex, if not *potus et ertex*, said that the whole British Turf, King, Lords, and Commons, were a d—d set of swindlers together, which showed that they knew nothing about the business. In fact the world was utterly in the dark for the present about Flying Scud, excepting that dead or alive he still stood at about ten to one.

CHAPTER IV.

A SPORTING LAWYER AND HIS CLIENTS.

In a small country town, a short distance from Nobbley Hall, and half a mile from the railway station, which we call Middle-thorpe, there was a large and imposing-looking white house. It had several windows in front, and looked altogether honest and open to inspection, such as a lawyer's house ought to look. On one side of the hall were the apartments in which Mrs. Quail received the wives of the doctor, the curate, the principal farmers, and the head

4—2

linen-draper, who was also the banker. On
the other were the business-like looking
offices of Quail himself; a man well to do
and of good report, better even than lawyers in general; and, more extraordinary
still), in some things not undeserving of
the confidence reposed in him. The only
impudent thing about the house was its
very green door, with its very bright brass
knocker, which separated Quail the Social
from Quail the Affairé, or Official.

In that little office, three days after the
death of old John Sykes, sat Mr. Quail the
lawyer, his confidential man of business,
who had invested his money, engaged his
tenants, eaten his dinners, admired his
horses, and made his will. It was a dusty-
looking place, for no servant was allowed to
enter it excepting under the guidance of
Quail himself, who knew the value of his

documents and the intelligence and discre-
tion of his housemaid too well to trust them
together. He was a sharp-featured person,
with clear grey eyes, and his hair was beginning to match them.

"Come in," said he, hastily recovering
himself from a reverie into which he was
relapsing on John Sykes's affairs, which at
that moment were uppermost in his mind.
"Come in," and the office-boy announced
Mr. Davis. "Tell him to sit down in the
outer office, as I am very much engaged for
a minute or two."

Mr. Quail only wanted time for a con-
jecture, and the consideration of how to act
in certain conditions; so he soon rang his
bell, and the gentleman of whom we have
heard as Mo. Davis, which, by the way, was
an affectionate abbreviation for Moses, stood
before him.

Mr. Quail saluted him cordially, and motioned him to a seat.

"And what brings you here, Mr. Davis?" Mr. Quail never wasted time, excepting when he felt that he was better paid for wasting than using it. He spent plenty with John Sykes, who dearly loved a gossip, but had no idea how much it cost him. "You're here on business, I suppose?"

The retired tobacconist of the Quadrant, who found money-lending and racing more profitable than even his trade in regalias of brandy and soda, looked up at the lawyer almost coaxingly, and said—

"Vell, yes. When will the vill be read?"

"On Saturday, my good friend; but you didn't come here to learn that."

"How do you know that?" said the other.

" Because you could have found it out with much less trouble ; as soon as the old man's buried, of course."

" Ah ! you lawyers, you know every-thing. Vell, I didn't come here for that." Here Moses assumed a serious face, and put his question somewhat mysteriously. " Is it all right with the Captain ? 'cos I don't want to be put in the 'ole."

" Put in the hole ! What should you be put in the hole for ? You're not dead."

Not a muscle of Lawyer Quail's face moved.

" You know what I mean, Lawyer ; about that thousand pound that Goodge owes me —is it all right ?"

" Listen to me, Mr. Davis. We took your instructions ; you instructed us to sue Goodge." Here Mo. Davis drew a very

long face, feeling that he had been guilty of
a great imprudence.

"But you never let my name out. There
vos a third party, you know—a party as had
a hinterest in the bill."

"Well," continued Quail, without noticing
the interruption, "we obtained judgment,
and were about to issue execution, when this
sudden and unfortunate death of the old
man happened. At the moment it wouldn't
be decent to proceed."

"Proceed! no, I should think not. Stop
it by all means. He's my very good friend,
is Goodge. Poor boy! I wouldn't hurt a
hair of his head. Oh, he'll pay; he's honest
—when he's got the money. Issue execution! Vy, Lawyer Quail, vot a vampire you
are to turn round on him in that vay, just
ven he's got such a lot o' tin."

"As you please—as you please; only if

you don't turn round on 'em when they've got the tin, it's not much use turning round at all."

" It's a fine estate, Quail, and all in a ring fence," said the Jew, brushing off a little snuff from his shirt-frill, which, with his thickly-folded white neckcloth, gave him a most respectable appearance.

" What estate do you mean?" inquired the lawyer, looking as if he had lost the thread of the conversation.

" Why, what estate should I mean? The Nobbley Hall estate, to be sure."

" 'Deed it is. Four thousand a-year, and good tenants; paying tenants, you know. There isn't a bad man among 'em."

" Vot a unproductive neighbourhood to live in," said Mo. Davis, giving his broad-rimmed hat a turn with his broad-skirted blue coat. " Never gets in debt, I suppose."

"Only to lay it out on the land, or do a bit o' draining."

"Oh, that's not much in my line; but they might want a thousand or two, and if the per centage is——, you know——." Here he winked.

"Yes; they're pretty liberal—high farming pays—five or six per cent. we can get out of them."

Here Mo. Davis sighed deeply, once more polished his hat, and shaking hands with Lawyer Quail, turned towards the door, muttering to himself, "That's lucky: sue a gent vat has just come into his four thousand a year. No, no; that vould never do. I'll lend him some more."

Having quitted the lawyer's house, the old money lender took his way along some meadows towards the Hall, which, by the short road, was about two miles distant from Middlethorpe. As he wandered along, he pondered many things, and among others, the fortunate event of his visit to Mr. Quail.

He had no doubt that he would now be paid by Captain Goodge, any money that was due to him, and as that gentleman's erratic course of life was sure to lead him into fresh disasters, he calculated—not vaguely —on having him again as a debtor, with a handsome security to back him. He, therefore, proceeded on his walk with a sort of personal interest in the property, and commenced, in his own mind, taking stock of it.

As he approached Nobbley Hall, the water meadows had been carefully drained, and divided by high timber fences, over which Mo. Davis could with difficulty, see more than the occasional head of a young thorough-bred one, or a dam grazing in her paddock, with a foal of six weeks or two months old, at her feet. He saw that these were, however, beautifully arranged; that each separate paddock had a large, comfortable box, with straw-yard attached to it, for the benefit of the young stock; and as the old Jew's love of horseflesh and knowledge of it extended no further than its capacity as an instrument of plunder, he knew as much of the value of the contents of those fields, as if he had closely examined them all.

The party which had arrived the day before at the old hall, require a short description. They had—with the exception of Mo. Davis—been accommodated at the hall, not without much surprise on the part of the old housekeeper, the servants, and Nat Gosling, whose respect for their late master

emboldened them to remonstrate. It was
unavailing, however, for they were there as
guests of the new squire, who only wanted
the formal recognition of his claims after
the funeral of the late John Sykes, to com-
mence a new reign. He had found a room
at Nat Gosling's for one of his confederates;
the major and Mr. Chouser he had taken
into the house with him.

There is always on the turf a class of
persons who are unique in one respect—a
community of interests. This community
of interests brings them together. However
heterogeneous the elements, one powerful
leaven leavens the whole lump. But beyond
that, there are quantities of men on the
English turf who have simply escaped
kicking, because they have not been detected
in gross fraud by those who are capable of
performing the operation, or who dislike the

notoriety of horse-whipping even a swindler.
These men practise their operations with
impunity. They are not the intimate associates of noblemen, of honest men, or good
sportsmen; but they are obliged to be tole-
rated, because it is difficult, in a mass of
circumstantial evidence against them, to
establish a positive delinquency. They have
always sailed very near the wind without
coming to grief, and the consequence is
toleration.

As a boy, Captain Grindley Goodge was
handsome, idle, and dissipated; but he had
certain qualities which rendered him acceptable to men of better position than himself. His uncle educated him, and his
undoubted object was to make him his heir.
As he grew up, he displayed especially the
vices most distasteful to John Sykes: extravagance and dishonesty. He was placed

in a regiment ordered for foreign service, to
wean him from his haunts and companions.
He returned with a slur upon his name, on
some gambling transaction, and sold out.
It was a slur which could not be acted upon
openly; and he still enjoyed the protection
of a Club and the questionable countenance
of fast men upon town. His uncle still
made him an allowance, but declined to
receive more than a formal visit from him.
Half his talents in the concealment of vice
and rascality would have gained the man an
honest livelihood. He preferred tortuous
paths to straight ones; and was in half
the robberies of the day; but it would
scarcely have been safe to say so to his
face.

His friend Chouser was a fool as well as
knave, which the other was not. He, too,
had failed in gaining an honest livelihood

as a lawyer's clerk ; and finding the Turf a short and easy road to what he called Society, he adopted it in its fullest extent. To have booked a bet with a marquis was only exceeded in enjoyment by the pleasure of cheating him out of his money. He had supplied the necessities of Goodge from the pockets of an unfortunate mother and sister, and was now living in a piebald sort of manner as his henchman, half pigeon and half crow.

Major Mulligan was essentially different from either. He was a man of good family and position in a country where, to have worked for his bread, would have brought disgrace upon Castle Mulligan and all that belonged to it. He started in life upon five hundred pounds and an easy assurance, which had increased with his knowledge of billiards and the way to conceal his game.

At all games of cards he was an adept—
more than an adept. He was far the
cleverest of the confederates, and was possessed of a certain ease and polish in general
society which not even his *roué* life had
been able to abolish, or even much to de-
teriorate. He was the most accomplished
scoundrel of the three, and brought to the
general fund, besides his talents and
hardiesse, a most powerful auxiliary.

It seems that he had some heart, which
could be acted upon by certain impulses, a
thing to be said for neither Goodge, Chouser,
nor the Jew. Major Mulligan, who had
floated on the tide of society, by-the-bye,
since the day that he started in life on his
own account, had once had a sister. She
married a poor, but honourable man, who
had been simply ruined by Mulligan, by
backing his bills, and who died within a

very ace of beggary. He took some credit
to himself for having clothed and fed her
for three years, with her only child, a
daughter, and for having then followed her
to the grave. Strict analysis of the Major's
character, makes us think that there was
some alloy in this virtue. A sister in a
workhouse was not at all suited to his
notions of the dignity of one of the Mulli-
gans of Castle Mulligan; and, as his suc-
cesses had been beyond his expectations, I
might almost say his deserts, he extended
his benevolence to the orphan girl. When,
at the age of eighteen, she returned to the
Major's handsome apartments in the neighbourhood of Langham-place, he had cause
to congratulate himself upon the acquisition
of a companion, the handsomest, and one of
the most accomplished girls in London.
From that day, his dinners, his card parties,

his little suppers, were more *recherché* than ever; and the line that was held out to them in so agreeable an addition, brought troops of men of every class to his table. A very beautiful face, which smiles over the transaction, robs the pain of disturbing a hundred or two at *écarté* or billiards of half of its sting, especially when it insures the pleasure of revenge.

The *sobriquet* of these four men was not legion, but quadruped, and the etymology of the word, if we substitute "legs" for "feet," makes its application more witty than complimentary.

CHAPTER V.

MASTER AND MAN.

CAPTAIN GRINDLEY GOODGE walked up and down the morning room, which he perfumed with one of the very best Colorados that Mr. Goode, of the Poultry, could supply. He was one of those persons who might have boasted, like old Lord Spatchcock, Woodbie's uncle, on his death-bed, that he had never denied himself anything, excepting, he might have added, the luxury of an honourable action. He was exceedingly cheerful; and as he surveyed the ample

hall, the substantial dining and breakfast
rooms, with their old-fashioned but massive
wainscoting and furniture, and looked
through the mullioned windows on the fair
prospect beyond, he thought of the remains
of his uncle, old John Sykes, which were
lying in a distant part of the house, only as
an incumbrance which would be removed
to-morrow. In the park he caught sight of
something which would have chased away
any feeling of respectable regret for the old
man. Three or four yearlings were being
led about by as many boys, while in the
centre of them stood the man with whom
the reader has been already made acquainted
as Tom Meredith, the tenant farmer and
trainer, and the late owner's right-hand
man. He walked towards the party.

"Well, Mr. Meredith, I hope the young
ones are going on to your satisfaction."

" Perfectly so, Captain Goodge," said the trainer, not touching but raising his hat, with perfect politeness and self-possession. " We have a nice lot. That third colt is in the Derby of '6 —, and as the Newminster and Arrow blood seems to nick ——"

" If it's not an impertinent question, might I ask how long you have been a tenant of my late uncle's ? As you've had the best farm on the estate you ought to have driven a prosperous business."

" Tolerable. The fact is, Captain Goodge, that your uncle treated me with great kindness. The farm was let to me upon an average of two pounds an acre, though it's worth four in the market; for part of it is accommodation land, and as to the buildings, why, I was never pressed about them, for they were built at my expense."

" Then you're a fortunate man, Mr.

Meredith. I'm sorry to say that the rents must be raised after the next half-year, as I'm not so able to afford reductions as my uncle might have been; and as to the paddocks, I intended to take those into my own hands."

And although the Captain had said a hard thing, he looked evilly, as if it had been done designedly.

"The paddocks," replied the other. "I shall be prepared to pay a full rental for the land, sir, though your uncle has promised me a lease over and over again, of the whole. But the paddocks. I hardly see how I'm to get bread without them; for the little I ever had has been laid out on them."

"Well, Mr. Meredith, I'm a poor man, or shall be for some time; and I must have the paddocks for my own use."

" You'll want a trainer."

" I should like a private one. I know the rascality of the world."

Indeed, he did; report said so, and Tom Meredith was of report's opinion.

" I should be happy to give up all other masters, if you desired it; and as I know the horses——"

" Unfortunately, I have already engaged a trainer."

" You've been quick about it, sir."

It was impossible to conceal from himself, or from the Captain, that he detected the falsehood.

" But now we've settled that business, just let me see the horses."

And they proceeded to inspect the stock which was on the premises.

" And now for the Criterion colt, Flying Scud; we'll look at him."

Tom Meredith looked up sharply, and hesitated; but, apparently making up his mind, said, "Then we must go to the other stable. It's a little way from the house—near my own cottage."

The Captain prepared to accompany him.

"And what do you think of him?"

"I think very well of him." For Tom would have declined answering altogether (which a trainer or owner ought to do) rather than have told a lie. "I think very highly of him indeed."

"It's a pity he won't go for the Derby," said the Captain, maliciously.

Tom stared at him and repeated the words slowly, "but he will go for the Derby."

"I should like to lay a thousand to ten about it."

" I shouldn't like to rob you, or I should say ' done,' " replied Tom.

" The nomination's void. Besides, you know he was beat in his trial; though I suppose you'd have persuaded me to back him."

Tom Meredith turned suddenly round, and confronted Captain Grindley Goodge.

The two men were worth looking at as they stood facing one another—the gentleman and the trainer. On the one side, the pretender to fashion, the amateur sportsman, gloved, paletôted, chaussé from Paris, and clothed with sedulous care; on the other, the true lover of a horse, the healthy, hardworking farmer, clothed in fustian, and apparently indifferent to all ornament save personal cleanliness. Both were goodlooking. The one neatly formed, with a lithe, active-looking body, and dark, hand-

some features, with a cold, cautious look,
and closely compressed lips, which opened
only to sneer or to show his teeth, of a
sharp, fox-like shape and dazzling white-
ness; the other, a fine, handsome, powerful
young man, of great frame, set off by no
advantages, with fair hair, and a clear,
wholesome complexion, clean shorn, and of
a most honest and open countenance. Captain Grindley Goodge, in spite of his good
looks and good clothes, might have been
"nobody;" Tom Meredith, in spite of his
bad ones, could not help looking like
"somebody."

"First let me set you right," said Tom,
deliberately. "The nomination is not void,
for the colt is mine until after the Derby.
I'd a fancy for the strain, for the grand-
dam belonged to my uncle, whose ancestors
lived here for something like four cen-

turies; and your uncle gave me the nomination while the mare was in foal, and paid for it in my name. He was generous enough, too, to promise the keep for him, and in the event of his winning the Derby, he was to have half the stakes. I shall think it my duty to pay that to his residuary legatee."

Here the captain condescended to laugh, and added, carelessly enough—

"I presume you have all this in black and white."

"Your uncle's word, sir, was as good as his bond, and so is mine. If not, the nomination speaks for itself."

"As his trainer——" recommenced Captain Goodge.

"Flying Scud will be trained and run by me until after the Derby. You will then do as you please by the horse. I see, Cap-

tain Goodge, you've been following your
betters in attempting to get information by
a means which would have subjected you
to a notice of dismissal from Newmarket.
Take my advice: back the horse if you
think him good enough. He'll have an
honest man on him and about him; and
don't you go so far north on a touting
errand again, or you may chance to get
bitten. Now, if you'd like to see the horse,
I'll show him to you."

Captain Grindley Goodge, having ascer-
tained beyond all doubt that the trial, as
detailed to him, had taken place, had sent
out an extra commission to lay ten thousand to one thousand against him. Had
he believed one word of Tom Meredith's
caution he might have felt less comfortable
than he did.

When they reached the stables which

adjoined the trainer's cottage, it was found that the Major, Mr. Mo. Davis, and Mr. Chouser had sauntered up to find the Captain, and that they were now in vain endeavouring to get something out of old Nat Gosling. Nat knew nothing, and would know nothing; he believed everything to be fair in love and horse-racing; and though he regarded a direct falsehood as rather belonging to the southern stables, he prided himself greatly on the superior cunning of Yorkshire and the north.

"The Scud," as he was familiarly called in Middlethorpe and in the Ring, whenever his name was mentioned there, was a beautiful dark chesnut, with one white hind leg. He was the Bird-on-the-Wing out of Cloud; and his granddam by Phantom, the property of Colonel Meredith, of Nobbley Hall, had never been beat but once. Having

won the Criterion, at the Houghton Meeting, in October, he had been kept for the
Two Thousand and Derby. He was long
and low, with a handsome head and neck,
and full eye, which showed great temper;
his shoulders were beautiful, and his girth
deep, calculated for coming down or going
up the hills of the Surrey Downs; his
quarters were a little coarse, as he was
ragged-hipped, but he had plenty of width
and powerful thighs and hocks. Such was
Flying Scud, when he greeted the eyes of
the confederates on the morning in question.

"Oh, he's a beauty, s'elp me!" said Mo.
Davis, who thought this was a perfectly safe
remark.

"Arn't his hocks rather large?" inquired
Mr. Chouser, who knew as much about
horses as most betting men.

Major Mulligan said nothing; but believing his chance for the Derby to be void, and the bets off, secretly congratulated himself on having so formidable a looking candidate for the Blue Riband out of the way.

"He's eighteen pounds better than when he won the Criterion," said the Major to himself, as he turned to leave the box with his companions.

At that moment a girl of considerable beauty of the blue-eyed and golden-haired type, so amenable to the vicious propensities of a Lucrezia Borgia or a Madame Brinvilliers, and who appear to flourish wherever any poisoning or crime on a grand scale is to be committed, rode into the yard. She had a round, compact little figure, and looked, with perfect self-possession and some surprise, at the assembled guests of John

Sykes' next of kin. She seemed, however, quite equal to the occasion, and handled her good-looking horse, as he pawed, impatiently, to get to his stable-door. The Major took off his hat, Chouser stood with the impudence which is always at the command of an ex-professional lawyer's clerk, and the Jew was wondering, in his own mind, how long such a thing was likely to last in a farmer's family, without an application for an advance and a handsome percentage.

"That's a good-looking hack," said Captain Grindley Goodge; "is that one of my late uncle's, Mr. Meredith?"

"I've always ridden him, but as he belongs to me only by the kindness of my late landlord, I presume I must give him up. However, I'm too heavy for him, and as he's rather fresh, I got Miss Rideout to exercise him for me. She has ridden him chiefly for the last three months. She'll be sorry to part with her favourite."

"Miss Rideout—what, Kate?" replied Captain Goodge, hastening at once towards her, and almost anticipating Tom in assisting Kate to dismount. "Is it possible! but it's seven years since we've seen each other, Kate, and in you it has made a difference. You will scarcely remember your old playmate, either. I've been to India, and half over the world since then. It never occurred to me to ask old Nat Gosling or Mr. Meredith after you; I should have thought you were married long ago— as you ought to have been."

And Kate Rideout blushed and laughed, not altogether ungratified with the praise of a good-looking soldier, who was likely to be the landlord and master of her grandfather

and lover. For Tom Meredith and Kate
Rideout, though not absolutely engaged to
one another, were likely to be so when
certain conditions were fulfilled. Captain Grindley Goodge seemed mightily
taken with the pleasant reminiscences of
his childhood; and while Tom Meredith
and Nat Gosling showed his friends over
the rest of the stabling, holding forth first
on the merits of a filly foal, or a brood mare,
then of a Burleigh or Fawsley short-horn,
or even of a Fisher Hobbs, or Felix Hall
boar, he disappeared with Kate from the
scene altogether. They were found in the
old man's cottage some half-hour afterwards,
still reviving old recollections and earlier
years, when the Captain had nothing above
a white lie, as old Nat observed, to answer
for, and Kate was always begging him off
from John Sykes, who even then used

to express his suspicions of Grindley's futurity.

A word about Kate Rideout. Nobody, except old Nat Gosling, knew much of her history. She had been an inmate of his cottage ever since she had been a baby, having appeared there somewhat mysteriously some twenty years ago. From that day Nat's cottage assumed a better appearance. A respectable woman was engaged to look after the child; in process of time she was much at the hall, and was taken away to a boarding-school of tolerable repute, and considerably above the ordinary mark of a mere village education. And Kate not only became a scholar, so as to keep certain mysterious books connected with Nat Gosling's dealings with the Squire, but played and sang in her way prettily enough, understood something of

French, and grew up a village belle. She was the life and soul of the place, and everybody loved her. When Grindley Goodge was at his uncle's for the holidays Kate was his playmate, and people did say that the old man would willingly have seen them grow up together, and become joint proprietors of his property; but when the debts and dishonesty of the young man came home to John Sykes, and his black reputation preceded him wherever he went, he took care that they should not see too much of one another by his good will. She was a good girl, an honest, affectionate girl, and fit to be any man's wife; and when Tom Meredith hinted to his landlord his own hopes and wishes, John Sykes gave him his hand and his promise that he should not want a lease of his farm, or a friend at his back to accomplish the main purpose of his life. Death, not sudden but unlooked for, prevented the fulfilment of these promises, and the heir presumptive of Nobbley Hall had shown no great inclination to carry them out.

CHAPTER VI.

A SLIGHT MISTAKE.

" Why, master, what's the matter?" said old Nat, an hour or two afterwards, walking into Tom Meredith's neat little parlour; " you seem down i' th' mouth."

" So will you be, old man, when I tell you all. The rent of the farm is to be doubled."

" And you'll pay it, I go bail, Master Meredith. It's worth it."

" And the paddocks and training business are to be taken away."

"Whew," whistled the old man. "That's bad. Who told you that?"

"Captain Goodge himself. You know I was to have had a lease of the property this year: and I looked for it, Nat Gosling, not for myself—for I can't starve while there's honest work to be done—but for Kate. You know how she's been brought up, and though I believe in her love for me, I can't ask her to share a labourer's cottage, when she's been taught to expect the comforts of an independent home. It's beginning life again, Nat, and though we're still young, we're too old for that." And Tom Meredith looked doleful enough.

"I can't believe it," replied the old stable-man, taking three or four sententious whiffs at his pipe, by way of consolation. "He was always a bad boy—a lying young rascal as ever lived, but he was no that malicious to rob a man of his bread. He don't like none o' your name, mayhap, for it partly puts his pipe out; but he was fond of Kate, and when he knows the truth, he won't be hard on you. I dare say we've put him in the hole, too, about t' Scud, for he thought he was his own, and these d—d scoundrels can make more by losing, than by winnin', you see. Howsomdever, cheer up, Master Meredith. Who knows what the old gentleman has done for us?"

"We shall hear the day after to-morrow, I suppose," rejoined Tom. "In the meantime, keep up Kate's spirits, and don't say a word to her about the business. I'll be down when the horses are done up, and I've got rid of the boys for the night."

Lawyer Quail had had liberal orders given to invite all the tenants to attend, after placing their old landlord in the grave.

The luncheon was to be laid in the old hall at three o'clock, when the will was to be read, and not only were the people to hear the last of their old master, but to be prepared for the reception of the new. Captain Grindley Goodge had not condescended to communicate personally with Mr. Quail on the subject, but his friends had been requested to transmit some directions to him on the subject of the property, and had most officiously sounded this flourish of trumpets in the saturnine lawyer's ears.

" Raise all the rents," said the iron-grey badger to himself. " Raise the devil! If Grindley Goodge wants to hear something to his advantage, he'd better not apply to Lawyer Quail."

But he listened attentively, notwithstanding. The arrangements for the funeral were in the lawyer's hands.

There are men who have a good, strong, wholesome belief, through good report and evil report, that everything that is, is for the best. All hail to such men! Theirs is a courage to be proud of. Men whom no doubts nor certainties of ill ever turn aside from the right path; who have patience to bear and forbear; and who are rewarded in the end.

Now Tom Meredith was a good man; no man better, as far as his light went. He was honest, affectionate, industrious, charitable; but he was not patient, and didn't think that stunning blows and heavy disappointments were decided benefits. So it came to pass, that when his affliction found him out (and it did so after a time), his valour resembled rather that of the wrathful Achilles, than of the patient Job.

Now let us go back to Kate. Kate was

by nature and education a thorough woman.
She was a sort of pet of the village, and I
never saw a girl in my life, with Kate
Rideout's particular nose, who was not flattered—rather unduly—by a little admiration. She had been accustomed to hunt,
and as she was always well mounted, and
rode with as little judgment as women
usually do; and as everybody knew her for
neither more nor less than a granddaughter
of Nat Gosling, everybody was civil and
kind to the girl. Even as she got older, the
young squires, and the fast men who came
from the barracks, thought no ill of Kate,
and if she couldn't have a companion or two
to ride with her, or see her on her way towards home, she was quite able to take care
of herself.

But beyond Kate's natural love of power
and admiration, she had a great anxiety to

make Tom Meredith feel that she had some
strength of her own to bring to the common
stock, if it ever should be their luck to come
together. And certainly the one I am about
to divulge was a great opportunity; she
was going to make Tom's fortune, whatever
might come of it, and she should reserve to
herself the pleasure and the time of telling
him so.

To understand the dramatic situation of
our tale, it will be necessary to understand
the situation of the three houses in question.
If straight lines had been drawn from the
hall to Nat Gosling's cottage, and from the
cottage to Meredith's farm-house, and again
from the farm-house to the hall, they would
have formed the three sides of a triangle, of
which Gosling's cottage would have been the
obtuse angle. Near Nat's house, and on one
side of it, was a thick plantation, with a not

very much frequented path and stile, run-
ning through it; the path, leading directly
to the back door of Nat's house, and used
only by the servants or stable boys in pass-
ing from one house to the other. In coming
rom Meredith's house to Nat's, the footpath
ran close outside of this spinney, coming
into the same entrance, and usually followed
by travellers between the two.

Day was waning, but it had been pro-
longed by a lovely and bright sunset, and
the moon was just rising in the opposite
quarter, when Tom Meredith started for the
old stableman's cottage. He was endeavouring to look his blighted prospects honestly
in the face, through the medium of a conso-
latory pipe, as he walked quickly on. In
every phase of the vision he saw one figure,
which, while it added poignancy to his re-
grets, gave fresh courage to his determina-

tion. He had just made up his mind to a bold fight with fortune, when he reached the corner of the plantation, within a few yards of the stile. His steps were arrested by the sound of voices which he knew. Yes, there could be no doubt about it, they were those of Captain Grindley Goodge and Kate Rideout.

Now Tom was not an evesdropper, and his first impulse was to have interrupted the conversation by breaking in abruptly upon it. Second thoughts—which are not always best—determined him upon halting a moment to make sure.

"Then you promise, Captain Goodge?" said Kate, in her most coaxing tone, and one which Tom knew well.

"Why should you doubt me, Kate? You know I'd do anything to please you."

"Ah, you gentlemen, you often say one thing, and mean another."

"Gentlemen, indeed. Where did you form your notion of gentlemen, I should like to know? Haven't I always been kind to you, Kate?"

And it is not to be wondered at that these softly-spoken queries should have caused a strong convulsion in Tom Meredith's feelings; so with trembling limbs and bated breath, he waited for his darling's answer.

"Yes, you have; and when others thought ill of you, and spoke against you, I always took your part," replied Kate.

"And I deserved it of *you*, at all events. So we shall meet again soon. Come, Kate, you must promise something on your part too, you know."

"Oh, Captain Goodge, you know we shall meet again. Isn't my grandfather one of

your servants, and arn't you going to live at
the hall; of course we shall meet again?
There now, you have promised."

The tone in which these words were
spoken was not such as to reassure a
doubting lover, and Tom Meredith got still
less of consolation out of what remained
behind.

"And now I must go. I wouldn't have
my grandfather know I was here for worlds,"
and she appeared to the jealous ears of Tom
to be making an ill-sustained effort to get
away. He moved a step forward, wrought
to a pitch of desperation, when the flutter of
her light dress appeared at the opening by
the stile; and as she turned for one moment
before coming out into the open path, she
said, "And above all, promise me too, that
Mr. Meredith shall never hear of this;"
Saying which, she ran—without looking

round—straight through the wicket that led
to Nat Gosling's cottage, and disappeared.

And that was the abrupt termination to
the trainer's happiness for many a day. He
leant for a second or two against the stile,
while the perspiration stood in drops upon
his brow. He removed his hat to catch the
cool freshness of the coming night, and then
hastened down the narrow path with an un-
settled purpose, but bent upon confronting
Goodge, who, he believed, had just commenced those overtures which would be the
ruin of Kate Rideout, as they were of his
own happiness.

CHAPTER VII.

THE MAN THRASHES THE MASTER.

The Captain, in the meantime, sauntered slowly back, puffing a cigar, and pluming himself upon the success of a villainy, which was as sudden as it was ruthless.

"Yes," thought he, "he may keep his farm and his paddocks, but Kate Rideout must pay for the diminished rental and my inconvenience. Who'd have thought the little minx would have grown up such a beauty? Julia Latimer, indeed! I suppose I shan't be such a bad catch now, though

7—2

as long as Woodie holds on, old Castle
Mulligan wouldn't look at a commoner at
any price. Why, Kate's worth a dozen of
her, and there's no necessity to be tied for
life to some piece of buckram of country
propriety in petticoats, which must be the
alternative of the proprietor of Nobbley
Hall."

I don't say his thoughts took this form
of words, though they might have done for
want of better; and they certainly would
have gone on in the same strain, but that a
heavy hand on his shoulder, put an unex-
pected stop to them.

"Hold, Captain Goodge," and at the
weight and the sound, that gentleman
turned suddenly round. They were just
outside of the spinney, on the side nearest
to the hall. The Captain's reply was at
least natural.

" What the d—l, sir, do you mean by this impertinence ?"

" Captain Grindley Goodge," said the other —his face livid with passion, and his words coming rapidly, but not very distinctly, while his voice trembled, and every vein in his body was swelling with the suppression of his emotions—" I know the difference between our positions here, sir, that of land-lord and tenant; master and servant, if you will, but I insist upon knowing by what right you—you——" he would have said " come here poaching upon my manor," at least, that's what he meant, but the phrase did not at all convey the strength or seriousness of his meaning. " You come here to insult a defenceless woman, whose position ought to be her greatest claim to your protection. I insist upon knowing your intentions towards the young lady with whom you have just parted."

It must be admitted that Tom had taken up a rather untenable position, and the Captain's temper, which was of quite a different kind, was not likely to forego any advantage he might derive from that fact.

"My intentions towards my servant's granddaughter? I don't know what you mean, Mr. Meredith."

And here Captain Goodge laughed, as if it were a joke, and showed his sharp, cruel-looking white teeth.

"You know well enough what I mean, sir, and you cannot well avoid giving me an answer to my question." Tom Meredith felt that his own interference was an absurdity, after all, and it did something towards abating his violence, though not his perseverance.

"If you're a gentleman, Captain Goodge, and a man of honour, you will tell me what was your subject of conversation with Kate Rideout."

"You seem to forget that I might be betraying the lady's secrets, as well as my own."

And here he laughed in the same irritating manner.

"I believe that young lady has no secrets from me," said Tom.

"The she's very little like the rest of her sex, of which I've had considerable expeperience. You forget yourself strangely, sir. I've known the young woman you are pleased to call a lady, since she was almost a child, and I see no reason why she should not retain some pleasing recollections of former days. I do, I can tell you. Perhaps they are reciprocal."

And again he laughed that mocking laugh, which said so much more than even his language, equivocal as that may be regarded.

The fact is, that Tom had no right to interfere, excepting that right which the impulse of an honest man gave him; at all events, he had never announced any other right, and it tied his hands, if not his tongue, for the present.

"Captain Goodge," said he, "if you mean aught but good by that girl, you are a villain. God knows whether my suspicions are just: if they are not, I beg your pardon; if they are, I'd make no more of tearing your craven heart out, than I would of cutting down a poisonous herb, or scotching a viper before it could do harm."

"Mr. Meredith," said the other, and nothing moved from his placid tone of

speech, so closely did he cling to the conventional superiority by which he was surrounded, " if you are about to become the
avenger of all the injured innocence of the
neighbourhood, and the defender of rustic
virtue in danger of temptation, you will have
plenty to employ your time and your talents.
As to Miss Rideout, she will neither thank
you for your interference, nor need your
protection. Stand out of my way, sir! I
wish to pass."

But the last insinuations were scarcely to
be withstood by a man of Tom Meredith's
temper, nor in his relationship to the girl
in question.

Instead of standing out of the way, he
placed himself in the middle of the path;
already his hand was on the throat of his
adversary, and a struggle—which seemed to
have no definite object but the gratification

of passion—was about to take place, when
lights appeared at the windows of the hall,
and footsteps of servants or labourers belonging to the estate, reminded both how
near they were to help or interference, which-
ever it might be.

It was pretty certain which way such a
struggle must have terminated, for Grindley
Goodge, active and well-built a man as he
was, would have had no sort of chance in
the gripe of such a fine, powerful fellow as
Tom Meredith, whose pursuits alone gave
him a physical superiority over half-a-dozen
such victims to enervating indulgences as
the Captain and his associates. It is only
difficult to know, when Tom had knocked
him down, what he was to do with the body
afterwards. As to the pleasure of merely
preventing his rival from going to the hall,
it was a very questionable one, and in

another moment would possibly have presented itself to Tom's mind in that light. The Captain's malice, however, saved him all trouble of self-restraint, and showed him far superior to the trainer in mental resources for injury.

"Unhand me, sir, immediately. D—n! don't you see that the scandal will become the talk of the whole village? You can't make the girl's character any better by such an assault as this. If you've no regard for yourself, have some for her." Saying which, Captain Goodge passed rapidly on, leaving all his venom behind him, and Tom Meredith planted, not knowing which most to wonder at—the girl's falseness, the Captain's coolness, or his own honest stupidity.

And so Grindley Goodge walked off; and, as when some pertinacious cur, not, indeed, utterly deficient in pluck, but rather of the snarling and passively offensive kind than of the open and boldly hostile, having been collared and shaken by a braver and truer type of the English dog, takes a farewell snap at the honest victor, and escapes, so did the Captain, as he departed, leave the most accursed sting in the honest mind of Tom Meredith, caused him much to doubt the policy of his conduct, and shook his faith not only in the woman he loved, but in the virtue of his own honesty.

If Tom Meredith had gone straight to the cottage and sought an interview with Kate or her grandfather, he might have saved himself and her much trouble. Instead of doing so, he walked back slowly and despondingly to his own house, and his thoughts were less cheerful than he had ever known them in his life before. Tom was a brave man, but he was an affectionate

and impulsive one—better at doing than
bearing. It suited his physique and his
manner of life ; and when he summed up
there was a nasty array of misery before
him. His farm and occupation were to go,
that was certain. It was hard to lose his
money, his time, his livelihood, but that
might all be reclaimed ; and, if all went well
with Flying Scud, he might be a compara-
tively rich man before the summer was over
yet.

But Kate's treachery there was no getting
over. They were as good as engaged,
though he never had spoken the words that
would have bound two honest people together for life. She was an idol Tom had
worshipped in his way, and now she was
fallen down and broken, and for whom—
Captain Grindley Goodge ! and Tom laughed
savagely as he thought of him. A mean-

spirited gambler, of whom all men, even his associates, spoke ill, and his confederates said no good ; a white-livered cur, who had not the moral courage to shield by a lie even the woman he wished to wrong, or had wronged. By a lie. For it seemed plain enough to the lover that his insinuations were but too true. However, come what might, there's an end of Tom's dream ; and as he entered his cheerless home, he vowed he'd follow his old master to the grave, and then pack up his traps, live-stock and all, and turn his back on the old place for ever.

And all this happened because an old fool like Nat Gosling could not hold his tongue.

The facts of the case are these. When Tom Meredith desired Nat Gosling to say nothing to Kate about his misfortunes, and

Grindley Goodge's intention to turn him
out of his farm, he did so with a design
which the old man was scarcely able to
appreciate. Tom thought that so sudden a
disappointment would make a painful impression if communicated by any one but
himself, and he, therefore, made up his mind
to break gradually to Kate the disagreeable
intelligence himself, as he should find opportunity. Of a participation in pleasure, or
sorrow, perhaps that of sorrow is the most
suggestive of strong affection; and mutual
consolation and patience more binding upon
hearts than all the joys of life.

To say that Nat Gosling was by no means
impressed with the same necessity for
caution or consideration is nothing remarkable; but the old man might at least have
obeyed orders. He had, however, his own
view of the case; and as he walked off to

his cottage, he only thought of the possible loss of a good master to himself, for Tom stood in some such relation to him, and of a good trainer to his pet colt. Not only had Nat made up his mind that the Scud was to win the Derby, but that Tom Meredith and he were sure to share the glory and some of the money. It must not, therefore, surprise the reader that cursing had taken the place of caution by the time he had reached home.

"So, Kate," said the old man, as soon as he saw her, "your friend, Captain Grindley Goodge, has given Master Meredith notice to quit the farm and give up the paddocks."

"And who told you that?" said Kate, rather taken aback.

"Why, Master Meredith hisself, to be sure."

" Did he ?"

It wanted an hour to sunset yet; and, as the girl looked out of the window towards the Hall, a sudden resolution took possession of her. She hastily tied on her bonnet and left the house.

The reader knows her errand.

CHAPTER VIII.

ALWAYS A BAD ONE.

THERE seems plenty of room for reflection on other things besides the uncertainty of life in such a meeting as that which took place at Nobbley Hall during the week of John Sykes's funeral. John, though he went by the name of old John Sykes, was not really an old man; somewhere between sixty and seventy, of an active habit of mind and body up to within a few days of his death. He was only ill a week, I think, altogether. His health had not been so good of late years; but as he, occasionally, took a ride to town and trotted home when he had had enough of it; as he still went round the paddocks every day, and sometimes saw a trial or a gallop under Tom Meredith's auspices, nobody thought much of his change of health. The fact was that he suffered somewhat in mind. He was a man of peculiar feelings, something akin to what a gentleman ought to be, and something beyond what some of them are. He was only John Sykes, and John Sykes was nobody; but he was proud of the name in his way; rather, I should say, of his own support of it.

From the earliest period of Grindley Goodge's life John Sykes had one fixed intention, and to it he not only adhered steadily, as was naturally supposed, but he made his sister, during her life, and the boy

8—2

himself when older, a participator of it. He had determined upon leaving his pro- perty to his nephew, with the condition attached to it, that he should change his name to Sykes. Young Goodge had begun life at the Hall as a handsome, reckless boy, with no particular faults beyond those which seem to belong to remarkable health and spirits. He was noisy, idle, and somewhat overbearing, but none had detected symp- toms of greater vice. Prosperity, or the expectation of it, acts differently upon diffe- rent constitutions; and certainly young Mr. Grindley Goodge, when he returned from Eton for the vacations at Nobbley Hall, had been spoilt either by these expec- tations, or by the peculiarity of the edu- cation he was receiving.

Whenever John Sykes had any social difficulty on hand, he was in the habit of seeking one of two counsellors; sometimes both. Now, the proposed education of his intended heir was a domestic question of some importance; and he, therefore, had summoned to his assistance at divers times, Thomas Meredith and Lawyer Quail. John Sykes may be forgiven for having adopted the popular fallacy that a public school met all requirements, and cured all evils. His friends, whatever prejudices existed elsewhere, were not quite of the same opinion.

"Tom," said the old man, "you were at Eton once, for a short time. What's your opinion of it for my nephew? I suppose it's the only thing to do for a fellow of that sort. Everybody goes there."

"Well, sir, there are half-a-dozen different ways of training horses according to the tempers, constitutions, legs, and feet; and I should think boys are very like them."

That was Tom Meredith's opinion of the universal panacea; his own career having been cut short at that famous seminary by his uncle's misfortunes. Lawyer Quail entered more fully into the question, as became a subtle mind.

"Everybody says I must send Grindley to Eton, Quail."

"Why so?" says the lawyer, who knew that his Etonian clients were always borrowing his money.

"Because it will make a gentleman of him," said the uncle.

"I hope it may," said the acute lawyer. "My own opinion is that it will confirm whatever his previous propensities may be. If the boy wishes to be a gentleman and a scholar, he'll have every opportunity of becoming either or both; and, with your property you can afford luxuries. But if he has the propensities of a blackguard, there is no place in the world where they will be so easily confirmed. There is as good an opening for their display as for the abilities of a rogue in my own profession."

But he went to Eton and India, notwithstanding.

To say that Grindley Goodge at sixteen or seventeen knew nothing, is scarcely true. He was an accomplished gambler in a small way! understood cutty pipes, which he smoked at the village public, surrounded by an admiring crowd of village toadies; knew the odds at hazard; the winners of Oaks, Derby, and St. Leger for several years past, by which knowledge he increased his pocket-money by sundry half-crown bets with the

unwary, but self-sufficient young Yorkshire-
men, and made use of a vocabulary which
would have been considered gross in the
mouth of a Newmarket stable-boy, and for
which he had been more than once kicked
out of his uncle's stables by Nat Gosling,
whose sense of respectability, if not of reli-
gion, was shocked by his puerile blackguard-
isms and importations of blasphemy.

John Sykes knew only enough of this
to make him very angry : the more heinous
offences were supposed to be kept from his
knowledge, and the neighbourhood was
taught to regard the good-looking scape-
grace—for his worst enemies thought him
nothing more—as the heir of Nobbley
Hall.

His uncle, indeed—a man of great energy,
and believing that success in life belonged
especially to industry and honesty—was an-

noyed at his idleness, which he could not
fail to perceive. He was far from dull,
though ignorant of many subjects; and he
astonished some rather acute gentlemen at
his uncle's table, when about sixteen years
of age, by reducing to paper for their information the odds on three certain horses
against the field, and one of them especially,
by offering to lay them. His debts had
several times been paid, by those sort of in-
stalments which satisfy the creditor only
temporarily; so that when the boy left
Eton, what with the lies he had already told
to diminish their amount, and the rascalities
of which he had been guilty to evade their
payment, even when the money had been
supplied, he was an accomplished swindler,
and in the hands of the Jews.

This boy had been a bad investment for
the old gentleman, who desired to hand

down a name untarnished to his poste-
rity.

Then he went into the army, and in due
time he returned from India, having been
allowed to sell out, only because some dis-
graceful scenes of unfair gambling could not
be brought home so as to convict; though
courts-martial are not remarkable for scru-
ples on that score. Since Grindley Goodge's
return his visits had been at first frequent
enough at Nobbley. As he became more
and more involved in transactions and society reflecting no great credit on him, he
was a less frequent visitor. During the last
twelve months he had scarcely seen his
uncle at all, and his death was a remarkable surprise to him, and, in his position,
no unpleasant termination to their inter·
course.

Who's to remember such a trifle as a debt

of gratitude for education, food, money—
gratifications of sense, and an allowance,
which, if not very large, was at least regularly paid?

There could be no doubt that with Grindley Goodge's tastes the last article in this
budget was an absurdity. The allowance
was sufficient for existence, as he remarked,
but not for life; and as once a broken-down
captain, a ruined gentleman, a spendthrift
exquisite, before committing suicide, went
on the road, so now the bankrupt of every
degree, to recruit exhausted finances, or to
supply deficiencies, before the consummation
of all follies, goes upon the turf. Grindley
Goodge had early taken to this way of life,
for it presented features of great interest
and advantage to him, independently of the
mere means of living. Was he not to be
the Squire of Nobbley some day ?—and was

Kate took to her work and old Nat to his pipe; and they both of them listened for the knock at the door, or the opening of the latch, which they expected, but which did not come.

CHAPTER IX.

NEITHER of them said much about the absence of Master Meredith, as the old groom was accustomed to call him; but in the midst of their conversation on indifferent subjects, their minds were certainly occupied with the trainer's non-appearance. At first old Nat thought he might have been detained later than usual, looking over his accounts—a business which Nat Gosling regarded as requiring much time and exercise of patience. Still he was not usually so late; and nothing but innate delicacy for Kate's feelings prevented an explosion on the part of the old man.

Kate held her peace and wondered. The disappointment was sore to her, however; for prudence was the very last of the virtues she possessed, and in spite of her grandfather's caution she certainly meant to have given Tom Meredith a hint of the good things in store for him.

"Why should he be made uncomfortable an hour longer than it was necessary. Captain Goodge had faithfully promised that he should have the lease of the farm and the paddocks; and though he had never said so, she knew very well that she would be asked to share them. It would be very hard to keep the secret from him, after all."

But ten o'clock came, and old Nat went off to bed after his supper; and then she saw that her resolution would not be taxed that night. She almost cried, as she lay down at last, and accused him of cruelty—a fine moonlight night like this, too. What was the reason of it?

In the meantime, the object of her speculations was at home, filling his own mind with gloomy forebodings as to his future, and miserable at the supposed destruction of his hopes.

At one time he longed to start off and accuse her of her fickleness, to warn her of her folly, to learn how far she was guilty of deceiving him from herself, if she had honesty enough to tell him, and then to take leave of her for ever. He should be off in a day or two, and they'd soon forget him.

9—2

He had half made up his mind to this course, and was about taking his hat down, when a knock at the door came sharply and unexpectedly upon him, and he heard a man's voice asking for him in the passage. Tom opened the door, and Mr. Quail appeared, unburdening himself of his great-coat.

"Come in, Mr. Quail," said he, for he had a very good opinion of the lawyer for one of his class; "I can guess your business. He hasn't let the grass grow."

"Yes, yes; well, it's not difficult to guess, for of course you know the funeral takes place to-morrow; and as I shall be pretty busy in the morning, I thought I'd run in this evening and smoke a cigar," which he had been doing ever since his arrival. "And how do the young 'uns go on, Mr. Meredith? That's a very nice Derby colt of yours. He's a good deal improved since he won the Criterion."

Lawyer Quail was a bit of a judge.

"I think he is, considering the time of year. My opinion is that he'll improve more. I don't tell everybody so."

"A nod's as good as a wink to a blind horse, Mr. Meredith. I remember the grand-dam—he comes of a staying family."

"I'm glad to hear it. There are very few of them left."

"Yes, poor old man. John Sykes would have been glad to have seen the Two Thousand in his pocket, and then he'd have looked after your interest in the Derby. You've lost a good friend!"

"I have; and they're scarce articles, as well as the stayers."

"Don't say that, Meredith; you're out

of sorts, and I'm surprised at it to-night.
You're to see the last of your old friend
to-morrow. I came to tell you we start
punctually at 11.30. The luncheon is at
one, and we must read the will as soon
after as may be. It's not a long one; but
he's remembered them all."

Here Lawyer Quail gave a more pro-
longed puff than usual.

"I don't doubt it," said Tom, gloomily.
"I shall be at the funeral, of course, but
you'll excuse me if I don't come down to
lunch."

"But you must come; you can't absent
yourself without very curious remarks.
There, I can't say anything, but it's your
duty, Mr. Meredith. All the tenants are
invited. It was the old gentleman's special
request. You know he told you you'd be a
legatee, and — and — I say," here Quail

buttoned up his pocket, and slapped his thigh, as much as to say, it's time to hold my tongue ; " but you must come."

"And I tell you that Captain Grindley Goodge——"

" D—— Captain Grindley Goodge ! He's next of kin, that's true; and he's chief mourner, and so forth ; and let him sit at the top of the table, and be d——d to him. I suppose he's been at you about the farm, eh? He sent some of his infernal toadies and confederates over to me about it, but he didn't get much out of me. When he's taken possession under his uncle's will, he can do as he likes at Nobbley ; but I know what's what, and they can't get on without me, nor I without you to-morrow, so you'll come down to lunch. And now give me a glass of your good ale, for I'm thirsty."

Then Tom essayed in vain to tell Mr. Quail about his meeting with Grindley Goodge, but seeing he could not do that without compromising Kate, he fell back upon the refusal of the lease. Upon which the lawyer held forth for another hour, swearing away at selfish landlords, careless tenants, bad laws, and sudden deaths, till eleven o'clock at night; by which time he had convinced Tom Meredith that it was a great duty to society to appear at the head of the tenants to-morrow, and he might "hear of something to his advantage." So Mr. Quail, lighting one more cigar, set out for a moonlight walk home, much relieved in his mind that he had gained his point.

If I were writing a three-volume novel (and I never could understand why that mystical number should have been so generally applied to light literature), there is here a fine opportunity for digression on various subjects connected with our interest in this world after we have gone to another.

On that certain morning appointed for his funeral, old John Sykes must have looked with some surprise, not to say disgust, upon the proceedings of the gentleman who was about thus hastily to leap into his seat.   Instead of a house of mourning, except in the case of a faithful retainer or two, Nobbley Hall was becoming more and more cheerful, as the screwing-down and carrying-out process, which had been going on for the last two or three hours, progressed.

"Let me congratulate you, Grindley," said his friend Mr. Chouser, nearly severing his head from his body with affectionate

warmth, as he took his seat at the breakfast table, whose cold baked meats alone
would have made the late master's scalp
creep with trepidation. "At length the
auspicious day has arrived when the
Chinese proverb would tell you your spoke
on the wheel of fortune was uppermost.
Egad! the last of the late tenant is just
gone down stairs, and Nobbley Hall is
tangible."

"Are you thinking about your seven
hundred?" said the master. "You may
congratulate yourself, Chouser, quite as
much as me."

"Nonsense," laughed the other, with
his mouth full of *paté de foie gras*, which
had been supplied for the chief mourner by
Fortnum and Mason. "I never doubted
about that. There'll be a clearance of
timber, I suppose?"

"At the earliest opportunity. What's been done about the Scud?"

"Nothing at all," said the Major. "He's scratched, of course, so I never looked. Rasper is first favourite for the Guineas, I see; the Scud not mentioned, —so it's all right. Only one bet about the Derby — a thousand to ten against Mosquito. Anyhow, we'd have made a good thing of it if the old gentleman had outraged Providence by living till it was over. Mo.'s information among the touts is first-rate." And then commenced again the knocking and hammering so terrible to some ears, so innocuous to others.

"Hallo!" said the Captain, "what's that noise?"

"More screws wanted. Bedad," replied Major Mulligan, "it reminds me of that stable of Woodbie's.   It must be more like a coffin than anything else."

" And your own like a charnel house, Major Mulligan, from the number of dead 'uns to be found on the premises," said the Jew moneylender, opening the door at the moment, soon after which they began to leave the room for their divers occupations.

CHAPTER X.

"Sorrow is dry." It is rather characteristic of its emblems, whatever it may be of itself.

There is a persevering sort of drought which seems to attack your professional mourner, and renders a great consumption of strong ale and gin-and-water necessary to his existence—at least to his continuance in his normal state of being.

So it happened on the day that the late John Sykes was laid in his grave, that the

mutes and undertakers were entertained in
the servants' hall, while a jocund tenantry
entertained each other below the salt, in the
old-fashioned dining-room of Nobbley Hall.
Above the salt sat the heir-at-law and his
friends, who managed to find their way to
the luncheon, with the clergyman of the
parish, the doctor, Mr. Quail, the lawyer,
and a distant relative or two of the late
proprietor.   The lower end of the table was
occupied by the rest of the company, and
though Nat Gosling was there, and the
humblest of the tenantry, in accordance
with the last wishes and arrangements of
the deceased and his lawyer; one, at all
events, was conspicuous by his absence.
Tom Meredith had walked straight away
from the dust that had been consigned to
its dust—no one knew whither.

There was no lack of creature comforts,

and if Grindley Goodge was anxious to make a favourable impression, he had certainly gone the right way to do so. The rubicund noses and purple cheeks of John Sykes's followers and bearers might have been—as we have seen—the signs of hardly-suppressed sorrow, but they were not entirely unlike those which strong ale and potations of sherry and port are calculated to produce on the *dura ilia messorum.* Indigestion and grief are not altogether unlike.

Their conversation had undoubted reference to the departed.

"So, of course, Master Maynard, t' colt don't go for t' Guineas," said one.

"Nomination be dead and void," replied John Maynard, sighing, and swallowing another bumper of port.

"Nor for t' Darby," remarked another.

"I didn't say that," says stout John Maynard, in reply.

"Why, nomination be dead too," says the other.

"I see'd un at funeral. Where be Muster Meredith, Nat?"

"'Deed, mon, I dinna ken," said old Nat; "but nomination for t' Derby stands good, and Flying Scud's a starter, if he's all right."

"And shall ye win, Nat?"

The old fellow looked round, and replied—

"Course we shall, if we comes in fust; na doubt about it."

And as there was a move at the top of the table, the jolly mourners at the bottom took up their hats, and bands, and scarves, and bowed a handsome obeisance to the rising sun.

Those whom it concerned adjourned to the library—a handsome room, with carved bookcases, and a large table. The room was surrounded with books, for although John Sykes did not read, he was obliged to have something in it; and he thought the assumption of this taste was far honester than a taste for ancestors. So there were no Monmouth Street Knellers or Lelys, only a handsome old setter or two, and some bobtailed race-horses and hunters, which had been sold with the bookshelves and the billiard table.

Major Mulligan must have been very fond of the game to have tried to make a silk purse out of such a sow's ear as that.

" You'll have a new table here, Goodge, me boy," said he, after making only one stroke, with an unpointed cue. That was on his first arrival.

"Certainly," said the Captain; and he nearly added, and some one new to play on it; for he was one of those miserables that have not even honesty enough to be true to their brother thieves.

By the way, that proverb about thieves and their honesty, seems to me of doubtful truth.

Tom Meredith, while half repenting of his design, or rather promise, made to Lawyer Quail, to be present at the reading of the will, was guilty of no disrespect to old John Sykes, or what remained of him; nor did he believe Grindley Goodge to be much worse than half the young gentlemen of England.

He had had no experience of good society, beyond such as was always representing it as very bad society, and all the conclusion he came to was, that the confederates were a bad lot—roysterers, gamblers, unfeeling and needy spendthrifts. That was all, and as to the winding-up of his malpractices by making love to a defenceless girl, much beneath him—as he thought—in station—well! really, it was nothing extraordinary in Grindley Goodge, ex-captain of some Indian regiment, and presumed heir to a very handsome rent-roll. It was only in accordance with his feelings, not his principles, that he determined to be beholden to him for nothing—not even a seat at his dead uncle's funeral feast. So Tom walked straight off, after the funeral, to his bachelor's apartment, which he had once peopled with cheerful thoughts about Kate and himself, to think how miserable one might be made by a vicious man and an inconstant woman; and wholly oblivious that there are means by which we may heap up much sorrow for ourselves, without the assistance of our fellow-creatures.

After a very melancholy mid-day meal, he sallied forth once more, to pay a farewell visit to Nobbley Hall, at the reading of the will.

At the end of a long and handsome table sat Mr. Quail, the family lawyer; and as he sat he looked suspiciously about the room, and then at the door, as if he sought something that could not be found. In front of him were his parchments, a modest-looking packet, secured with red tape, and by his side a tin box, with the name of "John Sykes, the Nobbley estate," painted in white letters upon the lid.

He was looking for something he could not find, and an attentive audience awaited the commencement of business. Captain Goodge occupied an arm-chair at the other end of the table, not entirely facing the lawyer, but with his side face to him, where he sat with his arm on the table, supporting his cheek. He showed less signs of impatience at the delay, than might have been expected.

The rest of the chairs were taken up by the poor relations, and some friends and servants of John Sykes. The confederates had been invited to be present at the coming triumph of Grindley Goodge. The poor relations were especially melancholy—probably at the recollection of their very distant connection with the testator (some second or third cousins, or thereabouts), and highly distasteful to Grindley Goodge, who had sedulously cultivated his natural disgust for respectable poverty. They were sure, too, to rob the estate of some trifling legacy, in which spoliation they would probably be helped by the old-fashioned servants, with Nat Gosling at their head. Considering the number of annoyances, Captain Grindley Goodge did not look more uncomfortable than might have been expected.

"Now, then, Mr. Quail, I presume we may begin, and get this part of the ceremony over—an eccentric notion of the old man."

"Ah.!—yes, certainly," said Quail, still looking about him—now into the box, now into the paper before him, but always with one eye on the door; "yes, of course, Captain Goodge, as you say," speaking very slowly, "it was an eccentric notion, this publicity. However, Mr. Sykes quite made it a condition that these good people should be present; and—ahem——'

"That will do, sir; the time is getting on—you had better proceed."

And Mr. Quail, taking so suggestive a hint, cleared his throat and began.

"This is the last will and testament of me, John Sykes, of Nobbley, in the county of York, gentleman ;" upon which followed that peculiar legal phraseology which is calculated to re-assure any of the survivors who may doubt the correctness or validity of form, but which would only delay me and my readers were I to attempt to copy it. It is sufficient for our purpose to know that John Sykes (the aforesaid John Sykes takes up more room, and is, therefore, always inserted at so much per letter) gave to the County Infirmary a sufficient sum to compromise any little peculiarities of early thriftiness, to the repairs of the Minster and to the Additional Curates' Fund sufficient to hedge on the rather illegitimate method by which he acquired his first great start in life, and hundreds enough to draw real tears of distress into the eyes of his surviving relatives, who, a week ago, expecting nothing, were now disgusted at receiving only five hundred pounds a-piece. There was an annuity of twenty pounds each to a housekeeper, butler, gardener, and second horseman; and "to my old and valued servant," continued the testator, "Nathaniel Gosling, I will and bequeath the cottage and garden in which he lives, and the sum of one thousand pounds, free from legacy duty; and from and after the decease of the said Nathaniel Gosling, the same to revert unconditionally to Kate Rideout——" At this moment the door of the library opened noiselessly, and Tom Meredith entered the room.

At first he was unperceived. Notice had centred on the fortunate groom, who manifestly was overcome by this surprising piece of intelligence, whatever his expectations might have been. Nat was a general favourite, too, with his fellow-servants, and received their whispered congratulations ; and there was not a soul in the house who would not rejoice in the good fortune of Kate Rideout. As to Captain Goodge, he was a little impatient at these heavy demands on what he considered his property, but sat, biding his time, in the cheerful prospect of immediate possession, and only wondering how long the list of old John Sykes's legatees was likely to prove.

The first person to catch sight of Tom Meredith, who had heard the last words, and now stood in the entrance doorway, was Quail himself. The lawyer looked round, and was manifestly disconcerted to see that Tom could find no seat near him.

"Give Mr. Meredith a chair," said he, addressing one of the servants present; "don't you see that he is standing?"

There were in an instant half-a-dozen at command; the lawyer himself rising with a deferential bow to Tom, and motioning to one near himself.

" Let him stand, sir," said Captain Goodge, rising too, whose attention was only just drawn to the new arrival, and whose sudden passion sent every drop of blood to his heart, leaving his face cold and pale, while his lips trembled with sup- pressed emotion. "Let him stand, sir, and allow me to do the honours of my own house," and he threw himself into his chair, turning his back on both lawyer and trainer. Quail said nothing. An acute observer might have seen a rather satirical smile on his closely compressed lips, which augured a long bill as the most effective weapon to the next of kin whenever the opportunity offered. He had, however, a weapon nearer at hand and sharper, so he continued to read since the interruption with a slower and more striking emphasis, which the dead silence consequent on Grindley Goodge's incivility made more evident.

CHAPTER XI.

THE words dropped out slowly and deliberately from the lawyer's mouth: "And, lastly, I will, devise, and bequeath"—and at the word *lastly* the Captain turned in his chair towards the lawyer, and the colour returned to his pale face—"to my friend and tenant"—here he dwelt a moment—"Thomas Meredith, of the Home Farm, all the real and personal estate" — Grindley Goodge was on his legs, with his black eyes gleaming like a demon, and the perspiration on his cold and clammy face—" of which I shall be possessed, or to which I shall be entitled, at the time of my decease, absolutely ; and I appoint the said Thomas Meredith, to whose family I am indebted for all I possess, sole executor of this my will——".

But Quail was not allowed to proceed. Captain Grindley Goodge, with three strides, was at his side. The veins were swollen in his hands and forehead; his lips, blanched with something more than fear—with the utter ruin of all his hopes or expectations, and contending with an aimless and impotent violence—with difficulty formed words, as he demanded—

" And is that all, sir? Is there nothing else ?"

" Nothing," said the lawyer, smiling blandly. It was his turn now.

"Nothing? You're sure? Not a co-dicil?"

He ought to have seen the devil in Grindley Goodge's eyes; but he saw nothing but his own revenge.

"What! nothing left even to yourself, sir? You've surely not forgotten yourself?"

"Stay, Captain Goodge; there is something more."

"I thought so," replied the Captain, with a sneer, which almost seemed to cast a shadow over his death-like features. "Read it, sir; read it."

The lawyer proceeded to do so, with the same placid smile as before: "And I revoke all previous wills by me at any time heretofore made; in witness whereof——"

But Grindley Goodge's hopes and patience were alike gone, and, with one violent blow in the face, he felled Quail

to the ground, saying, with horrible
oaths—

"D—— you, you scoundrel! this is your
doing, with your friend Tom Meredith!
What does he pay you for your share in the
transaction?"

And so far had he got, and in that strain
was he proceeding, when the real master
of the house found it necessary to interfere.

"Silence, sir!" said Tom Meredith, coming forward, even in the midst of his astonishment. "You've committed an assault
for which you will doubtless have to answer. Whatever sympathy I might have
felt for your disappointment—and you deserved some—is cancelled by your own conduct, and I regret that the first use I can
make of my title to your late uncle's property is to order you to quit it. Go, sir."

" You'll be prepared, I suppose, to defend

the robbery that, by some means or other,
has been committed—the advantage that
has been taken of age and infirmities, to
the prejudice of the real owner of the property?" said the Captain.

"That's right, Goodge—it's a robbery.
Is it the old man's writing? Shouldn't
wonder if it was a forgery," says Chouser,
exceedingly down in the mouth, but pulling
up his collars, and affecting to forget his
seven hundred in the losses of his friend.

"Oh, Moses!" exclaimed Mo. Davis;
"what villains these lawyers is, to be sure."

He, too, was more concerned for his thousand than for Grindley Goodge.

"Faith, me boy, you're right. The
description's wrong. Your uncle, was he?
Bedad, he describes himself as 'gentleman'
at the head of the document. He's no
pretensions to the name, I'm told—a mere

money-scraping, shilling-squeezing old vaga-
bond."

And Major Mulligan's left-handed compliment to the nephew was continued with
much the same judgment; while the lawyer
was placed in his chair, and promised Captain Goodge that he would hear more of
him at some future time.

"As it seems to me that Captain Goodge
and his friends have nothing more to do
here," said Tom, "at the risk of seeming
inhospitable, I am obliged to defer the
pleasure of their company to another time.
All particulars and opportunity will be
given them for proving their claim, if any
exists, by an application, through their
lawyer, to Mr. Quail."

Which speech only goes to show how
much too honest was Tom Meredith to
fight a battle in a court of law, and how

little he knew of Mr. Quail, if he imagined that he would have given them, of either one or the other, more than he was obliged.

In this simple, but decisive manner, Captain Goodge, Major Mulligan, Mr. Chouser, and their Jew associate were dismissed from the home of the late John Sykes.

When the first of these gentlemen was turned loose on society by his uncle's will, that philanthropic old gentleman had no idea of the mischief he had done. He had been subscribing to hospitals and curates' aid societies, for the benefit of his fellow creatures, with his left hand, while, with his right, he had dealt them such a blow as would be received by the liberation, among patients and pastors, of a man-eating tiger.

It was quite certain that any good reso-
lutions which might have been formed by
Grindley Goodge, with four thousand a
year, were only conditional on that great
incentive to cleanly living; and when all
expectation of wealth was gone—nay, when
the very jaws of penury were opening to
receive him—he was not likely to forego,
or to modify, any of those means by which
skilful experimentalists open the British
oyster.

From that day affairs were changed at
the hall. Tom Meredith entered upon a
rôle which he was well fitted to fill—not so
much, perhaps, by his education as by
certain inherent qualities, which reverses
and a manhood of industry had rather
served to strengthen than to confine or
disguise.

One thing was remarkable — that his

11—2

spirits, before so good and full of animation, were gone with his accession to fortune. He had become reserved, silent, less appreciative of a country life, and careless of the duties it involves. This was, indeed, the reverse of what men expected at his hands. The only thing that seemed to interest him particularly was his stud. He put his horses into the hands of an experienced servant, on whose honesty as well as knowledge he thought he could rely, and continued to superintend their preparation himself as jealously as when it was a duty. As he said, he thought that Nat Gosling, with himself, would be quite a match for the machinations of the enemies of Flying Scud, and would, perhaps, bring some of those to grief who had been relying on undeniable information.

As to the horse himself, the facts of the

case were soon known. The death of John Sykes compelled his retirement from the list of candidates for the Guineas ; but as the nomination for the Derby was that of one Thomas Meredith, the horse stuck persistently in the list of starter for the Blue Riband of the Turf. As the peppering which ensued upon the presumption of the trial was judiciously administered, and as the confederates managed their business remarkably well, they were enabled to lay about fifty thousand to win about five—a matter of no importance to such professional talent, which regarded the five thousand as a certain bonus, and the horse, as far as winning was concerned, as good as dead.

Since the evening on which Tom Meredith had overheard the equivocal expression of regard and mutual understanding between Kate Rideout and Grindley Goodge, he had neither been to Nat's cottage, nor seen, even by accident, the girl whom he at one time certainly intended to make his wife.

Men are moved very differently in such matters; so diversely, indeed, as to set at defiance all rules of analysis of character. An impulsive man, it seems to us, would have gone at once to clear up the mystery; yet, impulsive men have sometimes great delicacy, and a certain shyness, or reticence, which acts as a counterpoise to their impulses. That Tom was impulsive we have seen plainly enough, and he jumped to a conclusion which was, as far as Kate was concerned, unjust; but he proved now to be shy and reserved, and held his tongue from that day. He might, under other circumstances, have made a confidant of

Nat Gosling, who would have lightened his mind in no time; but his accession to wealth, and his old position, was a bar to that confidence, and in his resumption of it, he found himself surrounded by acquaintances, but without a friend. Nat Gosling had his own opinions on the subject, of course, and they were not unnatural ones, according to his light.

Kate sat one evening, completely broken down, behind the stronghold of reserve, which was intended to hold out for ever; and, dropping her work into her lap, she said, " Mr. Meredith hasn't quarrelled with you ?"

Old Nat gave a start, looked at his grand-daughter, and said, " No : why ?"

" He's not been here since the funeral ?" replied the girl, interrogatively.

" He's a great man now, Kate; times

is altered," and he puffed forth a volume of smoke, which relieved him of some of his indignation.

" I think he might have looked in ; you used to be so much together."

" Aye, so we are now, girl. The young squire's as kind as ever his old uncle used to be ; and the colonel was a grand favourite about here, surelie."

" He might have come to inquire after me." And then Kate blushed at her own temerity. It was but a poor blind to her real anxiety.

" Aye, girl, but you see "—and the old man stopped, for fear of hurting the girl's feelings—" he's had much to do, and to think on."

" If you mean too much to remember old friends, I think you're wrong."

" Well, maybe he's a bit proud. You

might be, lass.   Folks never knows till they
be tried."

"It's not like him," said Kate, half
thinking aloud.

"No, it's not like him; but ye canna
tell till ye try.   He was the honestest, the
best, the kindest callant that ever lived;
but when ye put 'em out o' work, after
hard food and hard galloping, and gie
'em the run of their teeth in a straw-yard,
they always fly somewhere, and sometimes
altogether."

For the impression rankled in the old
man's mind that Tom Meredith felt the
difference in their positions, and that,
although well inclined to continue his kindness to Nat himself, he was unwilling to
run the risk of daily intercourse with his
grand-daughter.

Kate brooded silently over his desertion.

She was willing enough to make every excuse for her lover, but she could scarcely help feeling how different would have been her own conduct had fortune placed it in her power to befriend him. She little suspected that she was suffering now from her heedless, but well-intentioned step to do so.

CHAPTER XII.

THE MAJOR'S LITTLE GAME.

"BEDAD, it was a fine stroke, boys, anyhow, and it'll be that that will win the game, if I've any luck. But Lord Woodbie must give points; no man out can play the cannon game like him."

The speaker was Major Mulligan, and the language was addressed to Chouser, Grindley Goodge, and young Fitzwalter, Lord de Warrenne's eldest son.

"It's hard upon me, too, that ye'll be advising his lordship what to play for.

To be sure he knows better than you can tell him; but anyhow, we're playing for a stake, and you're not backing either of us."

Here the Major made two losing hazards, and won the game.

"That's a hundred off. I'll play you one game more, Woodbie, and you shall give me fifteen; come, double or quits, it's only fifty —but you're too good, ye know you are : and I can't afford more."

And the Major gave a baulk.

"Come, Major," said Lord Woodbie, " I can't give fifteen, but if you'll make it two hundred up, and play for three hundred, I'll give you twenty."

"Three hundred, is it? I'll lose, and where's the money to come from? No, I'll play for a hundred, and you must get Chouser or Goodge to put on the other two."

After long altercation they agreed to take Woodbie's five to four, in hundreds, upon which the Major begged to be let off his stake.

" I'll play you for a pony, just to have an interest in the game, but I know you can beat me easily at twenty points, me lord, and I can't afford it. If I lose, I'll go up-stairs, I know, and spoil the supper party, after being spoiled myself."

At the same time Major Mulligan gave a sufficiently intelligent glance in the direction of his associates, who were with reluctance, accommodating Fitzwalter, who wanted to back his friend for a hundred, at three to two. It was done, of course, and it was not the only thing being done at the same time in the room.

The game began (it was in a large room at the back of the Major's apartments, well lighted, well ventilated, and free from intrusion) much in Lord Woodbie's favour. And as that remarkably fast young noble smoked a fine, full-flavoured regalia—without which, he averred, he could not make a stroke—and drank iced brandy and seltzer, without which, he also averred, he could not smoke, the game went a little in his adversary's favour at first, that is—for a break or two.

" Put out your cigar, Woodbie," said the good-natured Major, " I'm sure ye can't make a stroke in such an atmosphere as this, or ye'll have Chouser and Grindley, there, winning your money. I'll begin to be sorry I didn't double the stake myself."

There was a kindly, patronising air in the Major's address which was, doubtless, intended to allay irritation, but unfortunately, provoked it. Lord Woodbie was very young, very green, very fast, and wished to be thought faster; but that was not Major Mulligan's fault. Honest Hubert Mulligan couldn't help that; besides which, he thought he played billiards just five points better than most gentlemen in England; and Mulligan couldn't help that either. Perhaps it might be true, he observed to himself, but then he'd forgotten Ireland.

Lord Woodbie was a little irritated.

"Double it, then!" said he, gulping down a little more cold brandy and seltzer, which, however, did not allay his lordship's irritation.

"No, no; I'm only joking," and here Major Mulligan made a shocking bad stroke, and let the young Christ Church man in, who proceeded to score in a bold and tolerably skilful fashion, with an occasional fluke, and very much after the bold University pattern. The fact is, for a young man he was very fair.

Having caught the Major and given a baulk, he desired to back himself for a little more, and on more favourable terms for the takers. After some weak remonstrances and expostulations, he was allowed to do so.

" Call the game, Chouser," said his lordship after a time, during which he seemed to have had tolerable success, and one rather long break. " Call the game, that's a good fellow."

Chouser could hardly have recognised himself under the appellation, but he replied to it, " A hundred and thirty—a hundred and three."

" Who's a hundred and thirty ?" inquired Lord Woodbie.

"You are, my lord."

Chouser had not arrived at sufficient familiarity to dispense with titular distinctions, but by the easy process of book-making, and laying what he had not got, was reaching it.

"Then I'll lay another hundred even, Goodge," said his little lordship.

"Not I. You're in luck, and Mulligan's a regular duffer. I'll take a hundred to seventy-five," said the Captain. .

"Done—put it down;" and having swallowed a mouthful of smoke which half blinded, and wholly choked him, the little noble missed his cue, and Major Mulligan proceeded to score.

It was a great point with the Major, as of course it is with all judicious swindlers, —whether on the turf or at the billiard table—not to frighten their prey. Judicious

losing is quite as essential as any other of
the tricks of the game.   Flatter your adversary while you beat him in the long run.
The greatest rascals are the greatest adepts
at this graceful manœuvre, and the Major
was *nulli secundus* in the delicacies of cheating.

Having got within ten points of his adversary, he thought it desirable to play the
wrong game, for which stupidity he was
saluted with a shout of abuse from his
backers, Messrs. Chouser and Goodge, and
some favourable notice of Fitzwalter, as not
quite up to the mark, and an offer to go on
backing his friend Woodbie.   There   is
nothing so charming in the way of moral
felony, nothing so exquisitely satisfactory
to both parties, as clever legging at billiards.

It was becoming absolutely necessary to

play a very flattering game. At one moment the Major had almost determined upon
allowing the amiable youth to win. It
would be such a grand stroke, and really,
his colleagues were not half considerate to
him, occasionally, as they should be. It
was a great temptation. He might have a
private picking, which would well repay
him for his self-restraint, and he would so
like to sell those rascals, Chouser and
Goodge, who had got much more out of the
Cambridgeshire than they ever admitted to
him.

However, second thoughts about "a bird in
the hand," and "striking while the iron was
hot," proved more acceptable ; so he drew
gradually on, appearing to make a very hard
fight of it, and now and then—after a better stroke than common—admitting the soft
impeachment of a "fluke."

To do Woodbic justice, though not select enough in his company, he was a perfect gentleman, and when the game stood ninety all, he blew forth a fresh puff of tobacco, and prepared to play with as much *sang froid*, as if he had one sovereign on it instead of rather better than five hundred. And he did play, and having made nothing —but left the balls with a not very difficult cannon for Mulligan—he looked, with calm composure at his handiwork, remarking—

" There's plenty of room to go round it, Major, and then I shall go in and win."

As the Major felt that he had played his fish quite long enough, and that everything had been done that a proper amount of flattery could suggest, and with very excellent results, he took care not " to go round it ;" and leaving an easy hazard over the

middle pocket off the red ball, which he repeated three times consecutively, laid down
his cue, with the best perpetrated sigh of
relief that had ever been heard.

"'Gad, it was a near go," said his lordship, "I don't think I can give quite
twenty; at least, it requires good form."

At the same time he took out his pocket-
book, and having made a careful memoran-
dum of his losses, proceeded to hand them
over in notes, across the table, to the impudent sharpers who had pigeoned him. It
was all very well to speak of the confedera-
tion as the "quadruped;" it was quite clear
that it wasn't "an ass."

Major Mulligan was a great rascal, but
he could be—as he was very early in life—
a polished gentleman. Notwithstanding the
roll of his hat, and the roll of his tongue,
there were times when his manner was as

finished as that of the best class of his countrymen—which is saying a great deal. It was peculiarly flattering to young men, which is usually the case when the sympathies and occupations are alike. It was so now, when he asked Lord Woodbie to finish the evening in his rooms up-stairs, which Lord Woodbie—looking at his watch—was about to decline on the score of time.

" Miss Latimer will regret the loss of such an opportunity of extending her small hospitalities to your lordship."

" Miss Latimer!" repeated his lordship, with rather less of good breeding than his host. But he was evidently surprised into the expression.

"My niece, Lord Woodbie, who does me the honour of keeping house for me, as far as a bachelor's establishment admits of it."

And as he opened the door of the billiard room, Lord Woodbie passed out before him.

The wave of the hand, and the comprehensive bow with which—five minutes later—he presented his noble pigeon to the young lady, was worthy the best days of the late court of Pumpernickel, or of Bath under the influence of Beau Nash.

"Lord Woodbie—me niece, Miss Latimer."

Julia Latimer and Lord Woodbie stared with some surprise, and then shook hands.

"We are not old, but I hope I may say intimate acquaintances, Major Mulligan," said the young man, blushing slightly, which was scarcely perceptible, however, by the light of the lamp or chandelier.

Mulligan knew it well enough, but the needless display of knowledge is not characteristic of good breeding or high society ; so he had, as we see, kept that knowledge to himself.

"It will be a great honour that you should give us the opportunity of improving that acquaintance."

Julia Latimer herself walked towards the table without a word, looking steadily down upon a tea equipage which was standing on it, and offered Lord Woodbie a late cup of tea, which he took. Julia was blushing for her uncle, who she felt instinctively, was acting a lie.

Somehow or other, I think, if there had been a crooked and a straight path to the same place, the Major would have preferred the former. Practically he believed two sides of a triangle to be shorter than the third.

There's an English nobleman or two who

could tell you a tale about billiards in early
life, which would make you think twice
before you took to " knocking the balls
about " at a public table in a private room,
especially if you chance to be what is called
" sweet upon yourself."

CHAPTER XIII.

WE have not seen much of Julia Latimer yet except through the panel of a door. Let us look at her face to face : it is worth the trouble. No two women could be more different than she and Kate Rideout. The latter fair, light of heart and limb, not fitted for great hopes, nor to lead where doubt or danger were before her; nor to strengthen weakness of purpose nor guide and govern indecision; she was a tender and loving plant, whose strength

lay in her gentleness and love. Julia was
more than this. She was dark and rich in
colour, with large hazel eyes that owed part
of their power to the lids that fringed them.
There was no deficiency of tenderness or
trust, but an honest self-reliance in them
which might stand the owner in good stead
at need. Her features were straight and
handsome as those of a Grecian statue, but
not cold; such, indeed, as she might have
been had Prometheus breathed into her the
fire of heaven. Her mouth, which closed
calmly enough on ordinary occasions over
feelings which her words might have betrayed when scorn (and she was made to
feel it sometimes) curled her lip, was ex-
pressive enough of warmth for the most
genial critic.

If Julia Latimer was not so likely, or so
lightly, to be loved, she was a woman to be

worshipped. She would have stood by her
lover when all else had deserted him; she
would have carried him with her through
every danger; she would have shielded him
from his own weakness, have nerved him
with fresh strength for every encounter;
and if they could not have fallen or risen
together, would have sacrificed herself willingly, and all her happiness, for him.

And this was the woman who was compelled to witness the subterfuges of a gambler's life, at an age when other women are
not much more than out of the school-
room. Her days seemed to pass between
ill-disguised reticence, and openly-expressed
shame. Few women in England looked
more like a lady; none in her position
could have felt more like one. But it is
nothing extraordinary that she was as unlike the conventional woman of Lord Wood-

bie's imagination as Joan of Arc was unlike
a doll in a dog-cart. I don't mean to say
that there are not Lady Marys and Lady
Harriets as good, as strong, and as loveable,
as any beggar's maid in the kingdom. Many
much more so. But a Julia Latimer was
not the picture which the Lord Woodbies
are taught to contemplate as their future
ladies. Excellence is like a personal beauty.
Very high cultivation is apt to disguise it,
just as a course of callisthenics or crinoline
may divert or conceal the loveliest formation. As I love a highly-bred horse, and
expect more from him, so I regard a highly-
bred woman as capable of more than those
less highly favoured. But the *manège* may
do too much for both, and disappoint the
rider, when he sails out of the convention-
alities of the school.

Lord Woodbie was astonished. Here

was a woman, not his equal, as he would be
taught to believe, who was neither a pupil
of D'Egville, nor Maras, nor Hallé; who
didn't talk about the opera, or the queen's
ball, or even the drawing-room; who lived
with a gentlemanly old gambler in a quiet
street, and whose person owed little to the
aid of Emanuel or Maradan Carson for its
loveliness; whose grace, if it were natural,
ought to have belonged to a duchess,
and whose intellect was—well ! to tell
the truth, rather beyond his lordship's
depth.

So he fell in love with her at once. Not
like a boy—and he was not much more—
but with the ardour of a strong will; not
like a languid swell — nor was he very
much more than that—whose inane life had
been passed at Eton and Oxford in gambling and dissipation, in aping vices which

he detested, and in committing follies which he despised.

How could he help himself, and how could he have passed his time otherwise? Where had he ever seen samples of the old philosophers of the academies, who said all happiness consisted in pleasure—but that pleasure was virtue! Old Spatchcock, his uncle! who knew the name of every dish that Apicius might have coveted, and who could congratulate himself on his death-bed on having denied himself nothing in this world. The Duke of Cadwallo, his other uncle, to whom he was heir, a good man, forsooth! as proud as Lucifer, and as violent as a chained lunatic. A good husband, father, landlord, and sportsman, over head and ears in debt, hunting six days a-week, and visiting the kennels after church on the seventh; keeping a string of race-horses at Newmarket, betting and gambling all through the summer, and taking the odds on Sunday afternoon at Chantilly or Paris, while the governess at home was being scolded by the Duchess for reading "Lady Audley's Secret" instead of taking the Ladies Mary and Cecilia to church in the evening. Or was he to learn wisdom from his cousin Saunterre, who, with sixty thousand a-year, never had a horse, never played a card, or threw a main, but was half ruined by the opera-houses he had supported, and the ladies connected with them; who, and whose orgies at Saunterre Castle were the talk, not to say glory, of all the wickedest of the aristocracy. Or from that intolerable ass Lord Pinchbeck, who was clever enough to have invented a new brougham; and whose outside, from head to foot, had engrossed so much of his attention as to have left neither brains nor heart within.

When Lord Woodbie left Eton these were a few of the notable examples that surrounded his paternal, or, rather, maternal hearth (for his father had been killed in a steeple-chase a few years before.) Was he likely to seize upon the abstruse virtues of these people which lie beneath the surface, or to adopt for imitation and reference those glaring characteristics of fashion which come to the top? Who talked of Cadwallo's domesticity, who did not talk of his extravagance and gambling? Who talked of Spatchcock's refinement, who did not talk of his gluttony? Who ever heard of Pinchbeck's patriotism, who had not heard of his under waistcoats and hats? What was it in the world's eye that Saunterre was a man of exquisite taste and learning, to

the far-famed reputation he had acquired in
the French *coulisses?* So Woodbie, who
had great natural parts, great courage, great
spirit, great liberality, and unbounded belief in the honour of his species, who, in
fact, was a perfect English gentleman at
heart, had adopted all the characteristics of
all those whom an inconsiderate world had
endorsed with the name. Unfortunately,
he had an affectation, too. He was, as
Grindley Goodge had often told him, " the
fastest young 'un out."

A real talent for pace is rather an un-
common thing, and no man likes to be denied his title to genius. Now Woodbie
really had a turn that way, and was proud
of hearing it acknowledged. He was just
one of those men who might get over it if
he fell into good hands, which at present
was doubtful. He did so much of it with-

out liking it. His very cigars made him feel uncomfortable; but then Hudson and Carlin supplied him with whole hundredweights, and he plunged as far as the Poultry itself to ransack Goode's stores for the very largest and best Havannahs. He sat up all night, but he yawned most unprofessionally over the business. He scarcely knew one card from another, but played like a fine young English gentleman, to the detriment of his purse, and the disgust of his partner. He had horses he never rode, a yacht he never sailed, moors he never shot, and half-a-dozen boxes he never set foot in; and he backed bills, and raised money, and gladdened the hearts of the Jews to an extent that had never been heard of. He never said "no" to himself, and as yet he had found nobody to say "no" to him.

We have said that it was remarkable that this young gentleman should have fallen honestly in love with anything but himself; but more so with a girl like Julia Latimer, who had certainly but little sympathy with his apparent tastes and real occupations. But it is still more remarkable that such a passion should have been reciprocal. It is difficult to conceive that the lady should have been attracted by anything like Lord Woodbie as he has been at present represented to the reader.

However, there was the fact. Either that penetration, for which women are so justly noted, perceived something beneath the surface more worthy of respect and affection; or that blind and undistinguishing impulse known as love, and which lavishes itself as often upon the colour of the hair or eyes, upon the shape of a hand or foot, as upon heart or brain, had deprived Julia Latimer of those high qualities of discernment which she really possessed, and drove her, as the furies in the Orestean triology, upon her fate. Let us hope the former of these two. To hint that a coronet and twenty-seven thousand a-year had anything to do with it would be a gross libel upon women in general, and on Julia Latimer in particular.

Having admitted my inability to account for the first principles of this singular attachment, there is still no difficulty in explaining its rise. Everyone goes salmon fishing somewhere. It's the fashion to rave about it. Norway used to be the right thing to do, till the country was overrun with appetites, and half the English were starved. Jones always thinks that because Smith had killed three hundred pounds' weight of salmon on the Glommon or the Tana, he is sure to do the same; so he forthwith arms himself with all sorts of implements of chase and war, among them with a Runic dictionary and a Scandinavian vocabulary. At the end of a month he comes back, half-starved and very hairy, cured of Norway but not of fishing. Robinson had been there before him, and whipped every mile of stream in the country.

I need hardly say that Lord Woodbie pretended to be bitten with the salmon mania; and, having some property in that well-favoured land, Ireland, out at nurse, as usual, he gave up the Scotch moors, ordered his keeper to supply the family from one hill, sent down some friends to the others, and took his seat in a carriage to Holyhead, determined upon doing the patriotic landlord and the salmon together.

"What's become of Mulligan, Tread-year?" said young Lord Tippletoddy, to him of the Blues, one afternoon, sailing up Bond Street, about the time that Woodbie was thinking of salmon instead of grouse. "Have you seen him lately?"

"Yes—very. He won a hundred of me this morning at the club; never allowed me or Prendergast to have anything over a nine in our hands."

"And where's his niece, Miss Latimer?"

"She's gone to Ireland. I tell you what, Tippletoddy, my boy, it's a d—d lucky thing for you that she had no chaperone but that fat old woman in a turban to go about with, or you'd have been nailed. I never saw a fellow so spoony in my life."

"Well! but a fellow couldn't marry a woman without antecedents and that sort of thing, you know. She's nobody."

" I wouldn't advise you to let the Major hear you say that. He's descended from M'Murrough, King of Leinster, who ran away with O'Ruark's wife in Henry II.'s reign. Nobody! by gad! you'd be riddled by the clan."

CHAPTER XIV.

"Julia, my dear," said old Lady Mac Stickler, a relation of Julia's deceased father, "I've some news for you." Julia was staying with the old lady in the Tantudlem Hills, not far from the Woodbie property. "There's my Lord Woodbie arrived at Tantudlem, and as there's not a soul to speak to within thirty miles of the place but ourselves, we have asked him to make this his head quarters."

"I'm delighted to hear it," said Julia,

who found an Irish mountain even more stupid than the back of Langham-place, in the month of August, but who was obliged to go somewhere while her uncle went to Spa, Homburg, Wiesbaden, and Baden Baden.

So, within a few days of the time mentioned, he was installed at Tantudlem, and appeared so well pleased with his quarters, that he sent for his groom and the horses he had with him, and turned his salmon rod into a riding whip, and took to sketching the scenery with the ladies. That's how and where Lord Woodbie and Julia Latimer had met before, and where he and she seem to have discovered some hidden virtues in each other, which it will take our readers yet a few chapters more to appreciate.

While we have been describing these two

persons, more or less, and getting up an interest in comparative virtue, which more easily centres in vice and its exponents ; and while Lord Woodbie is renewing an acquaintance, begun under such favourable auspices for love-making—Grindley Goodge and Chouser have been in the billiard room, knocking about the balls and their friends alternately.

"Chouser, we must have that fellow Woodbie with us."

This being a supreme flight of audacious villany, beyond Chouser, he answered despondingly enough. "Must we? And why ?"

"He parts so well—so freely, that it's quite a pleasure to bleed him. I'm sure he feels it an accommodation to get rid of some of his money. Only he won't go on for ever. The supplies will come to an end."

" Well, but there can't be much advantage in letting him in ——"

" We have let him in," said the other, cutting short Mr. Chouser's unfinished remonstrance. " I'll tell you what; we must tell him about the Scud. He won't be frightened about that. There's many a fellow thinks nothing of robbing his friends about a horse, that would rather cut his hands off than cheat at cards, even if he wasn't to be found out. We're nearly blown on the turf, Chouser, that's the fact. The fellows are all so d—d suspicious, if you or I open our mouths, that we can't half rig the market."

" Well, what then ?" said Mr. Chouser, withholding his cue.

" Why, we'll get Woodbie to do it for us. He won't stand in with us, but he'll do it for himself and let us stand in with him. He's devilish proud, but he's proud of being fast, and he'll be very much flattered at having the first information."

"But the Scud will be knocked out, and we don't want that."

"Not if he does it. The ring think him such a fool, that they don't know he's any taste for being a blackguard. They'll only say it's a cock-and-a-bull story of his friend Cadwallo, who wants to back the horse."

So Grindley Goodge determined upon having a common interest with Lord Woodbie, which was a bold stroke on his part.

"I'll tell you something more, Chouser, if you'll listen to me. Funds are low, and want replenishing; and if I had any doubt of the trial, I'd poison the horse rather than he should win."

Chouser turned cold at the vehemence of his friend.

"Win," said he, "No; he can't win, can he? Why, we've laid heaven knows what against him, and the right party haven't backed him yet. We shall know when they do."

"Don't be alarmed; we shall know everything. I've a friend in the stable, Chouser; and as you're pretty deep against the Scud, you may as well know all. It won't take long telling. What do you think of Nat Gosling himself. He hates Tom Meredith almost as much as I do. He's thrown over Kate Rideout, and the old man won't forget it. Don't you think Kate would look well at the top of a table. We want a decoy, Chouser, and we must have one. Wouldn't you marry the girl yourself?"

"Marry !" said Chouser, aghast at the proposition. "I don't think I could, Grindley ; not even to oblige you."

"Don't be alarmed ; you won't have the chance. If there's no other help for it, I'll marry her myself. I think that would buy Nat Gosling, and then Mr. Meredith may look out for himself on the twenty-ninth of May."

While Grindley Goodge matures his plans for making Kate Rideout the mistress of his establishment, under one form or another, and the Flying Scud safe for the Derby, by his influence with Nat Gosling, or by one of the various means of robbery so prolific in his time of life, we must return to the new master of Nobbley Hall. That venerable pile, and sporting neighbourhood, was once more happy in possession of t' squoire, a thing they had not had since the break up of the Colonel's establishment. To tell truth, Tom Meredith had acquired some advantage by his servitude; for, had his uncle been able to carry out his intentions with regard to the Hall in Tom's favour, he could but have transferred to him an empty name and an empty house, saddled with every possible incumbrance in the shape of mortgages and debts.

The fortune left him by John Sykes was ample for all his wants, though not very large, and few men could have looked forward to a more prosperous or useful position, as a country gentleman, than he. But Tom was not satisfied.

Since the evening before the funeral, he had never ceased to think of the unworthiness, as he believed, which separated him from Kate; and, in proportion as he felt his isolation, did he become more unhappy.

At the very time when he could have offered her a home, of which any woman might have been reasonably proud, he was debarred from doing so by an unconquerable obstacle.

Tom was truly unhappy. He went about his business mechanically; and while his eyes were with Lawyer Quail or his steward, his heart was down at old Nat's cottage, whither his body felt a strong inclination to follow it. However, it did not do so, being under subjection to a still stronger will; and it is not to be wondered at that a man of Meredith's age and temperament began to seek solace in absence from home.

Meredith fought against his wish to leave Nobbley for many reasons. He was very anxious to do something for the tenants on his estate, who had had a hard time of it under John Sykes. There were barns to be built, and repairs to be done to the fences; new gates to be made, and timber to be valued; acquaintances to be made with the neighbouring squirearchy and clergy, who held out the hand of fellowship to a man who bore a name well known to all of them.

But still he wasn't up to the mark. He was sorely disabled. The blow came at such a time. He tried shooting, at home and with his friends. He hunted pretty regularly; but he was a big man, and not able to get together a stud towards the end of the season, and at a moment's notice; besides which, he remembered Kate so often when he had charge of her—how he gave her a lead here, and sent her round by a gate there, and how often he had taken her safely home to her cottage through the raw atmosphere of a November afternoon. Of course she wasn't there; for she'd nothing to ride.

He tried a visit or two; but he was awkwardly situated. He was not yet established as a county-man; he had to pay his footing by good manners, or liberality, or good looks, or public utility, which was slow work; and his position and tastes had never allowed him to associate with his former fellows, and now less than ever. He thought of London, but had not yet screwed his courage to the sticking - place.

Meanwhile, under the care of the new trainer, or stud groom, Joshua Masterman, and Nat Gosling, the Flying Scud continued to improve. The horse, like most of his colour, was a good doer, and required plenty of preparation; but as his legs and feet were like iron, and his constitution as sound and hard as his legs, and feet, the galloping did not hurt him.

The season, too, was inclined to be wet— at least, it had been through March, and we are now in the middle of April. The Derby has another six weeks before it, and as Flying Scud's nomination for the Guineas is void, he has nothing in the way of impediment to a sound and careful preparation for the Surrey event.

The library table at Nobbley Hall had the remains of a bachelor's breakfast on it.

The *Glowworm* of the night before had just reached the Hall, and gave the Squire the latest intelligence upon racing matters. He was astonished to hear that the Scud " was somewhat shaky in the market, and that there was a strong disposition to lay against him on the part of some gentlemen, who were generally well informed about North-country horses. He had finished, however, only a point lower than his recent price, owing to the support accorded to him by a stranger."

The paragraph closed with a hope that "the stable, which had hitherto enjoyed a high reputation for straightforward conduct, was not about to follow the example of certain parties, who were too well known to require special description."

Having got thus far, Tom Meredith rose from his arm chair, and with a mighty oath — for unfortunately he was not above swearing, under great provocation—rang the bell ; and as repairs had not gone on so swimmingly in John Sykes's time as they might have done, the handle came off in his hand : at the same time he kicked the *Glow-*

worm indignantly, forgetting that it only acted honestly in giving the information, and commenting on it.

" Is Nat Gosling downstairs?" said the new master.

" I think not, sir; but we can send the boy over to his cottage."

" Do so, at once; and tell Tape (that was the new man) to pack my portmanteau at once. I'm going to town by the mid-day train."

In the course of half an hour Nat Gosling arrived. Tom Meredith could scarcely regard the old man in the light of a servant, and it required some tact to know how to treat him. Nat, however, had brains enough never to take a liberty, for he loved the old name, and knew his master to possess the best characteristics of his progenitors; so that before others he

was essentially the confidential stableman ;
in private he was treated with more in-
dulgence. When the old man reached the
door he touched his grey hair with his fore-
finger, and then awaited his master's summons to enter.

CHAPTER XV.

AN HONEST MAN.

"You'd better take a chair, Nat; I want to talk to you."

In the days of John Sykes, Nat made use of the whole of the seat, leaning comfortably, though perpendicularly, against the back; he now occupied a narrow corner of it only, and placing his hat upon the ground, prepared to listen.

"I'm going to town, Nat, and wanted five minutes' talk with you before I go."

Tom then asked after a lot of yearlings

by name, and some decent two-year-olds, and the trial horse; but with these the reader has nothing to do at present. He watched old Nat's face very closely, who gave him a satisfactory account of health and promise.

"And what do you think of Mr. Masterman, Nat? The young things look well."

"Oh, he ar' gotten his head screwed on the right way, surelie. I hope he won't be too fond o' gallopin'. They new fangled notions don't accord wi' me at all." And Nat shook his head, not much like Lord Burleigh.

"At present, it don't seem like it. He's a steady man, and knows his business. I know it, too, you know; so I can answer for that. And now, Nat, how about the Scud?"

"Never was better; never see a horse thicken so at this time o' year. He grows the right way, Squire, down'ards. But what will t' Scud do if you goes to London just now? It's a ticklish time."

"I'll tell you what he'll do, Nat—he'll go up in the betting to a short price, and if Rasper wins the Guineas, you know how safe the Derby is for us, by the line we have. Look at that"—and he handed the innocent *Glowworm* to Nat Gosling, who read the paragraph with some difficulty, and then returned the paper to his master.

"I'd let 'em alone, Squire, if I was you. Only give 'em rope enough, and they'll hang themselves. I think I know whose doing this is."

"Yes, and in the meantime have it said that I got as much out of the horse as I could. The reporters don't believe in an honest man, Tom."

" Everybody does so; it's no use telling the world how good he is before the time. We shall let in the scoundrels who want to lay against him."

" And the honest men, who will fear to stand by him."

"If you go into the market, Squire, you'll get, maybe, 7 to 1 at four o'clock p.m., and he'll close, two hours later, at 4 to 1. To-morrow morning it'll all come out that the trial was a false one, and there's an end o' the fortune you may make if you'll only 'bide quiet. If they go knockin' t' Scud about, and nobody comes to the rescue—as they calls it—you'll be able to take 20 to 1, as often as you like, before anyone's a bit the wiser. To back the horse now is to play Mr. Grindley Goodge's game. He'll like to lay 4 to 1 better nor 8, a good deal, I take it."

"Grindley Goodge! what's he got to do with it?" says Tom, rather tartly.   ,

"You know Mark Heron, the biggest poacher in Yorkshire?"

"I do. What of him?"

"He's Grindley's tout. They two thieves war always too thick to please me. He was seen slinking off on the morning of the trial, when poor John Sykes died. He saw the trial, and thinks the horses ran at even weights. Now you know why Flying Scud has been unsteady in the market; the metal has been at work. They southerners think nothin' o' that."

"Then I'll put the metal right to-day, Nat; and I won't forget you when I do so. Mind, a man's a right to do what he likes with his own. He may run what trials he will, and protect himself from robbery and touting as well as he can—and he may hold his tongue. It's a small sacrifice, Nat, to the rascalities of the business. But if he ever tells a lie, or allows it to be told on his behalf (I'm not sure that he ought to profit by another man's falsehood), he's not worthy the name of a gentleman, and couldn't be handicapped with my notion of the thing, at any weights. I'm going to back my horse for five thousand between this and the First Spring Meeting, and a good deal more afterwards, if that comes off as it should; and I don't care who knows my opinion of his chance. I believe he'll win the Derby, and I shall most likely say so before I've been five minutes at Tattersall's."

Nat sighed profoundly as he took his hat from the ground, and rose from the corner of the chair he had partly and painfully occupied. His own thoughts were not profound, and may be simply expressed thus :

"If those robbers are disposed to knock down the Scud to 25 to 1, so much the better : and if the honest backers of horses are such fools as to listen to the rogues, and to follow them, let 'em do so, and find out their mistake. There are plenty of wolves in sheep's clothing who would not be the worse for the loss of their fleece."

So Nat Gosling reflected, but he had too much respect for his master to say so.

As the old man got up from his seat, there appeared in his manner some sort of disinclination to leave the room at once. He hung back, turning his hat round in his hand, and looking first at his master, and then at the pattern of the carpet, which

Nat must have, at least, known by heart. It was evident that he got up intending to go; but he didn't go as if he had quite finished his business—nor had he.

Nat had been for the last few weeks mustering up courage to ask Tom Meredith the reason of his altered conduct towards Kate. Not that Nat was really highly displeased at the change—as regarded the girl, though it went some way with him—but he wished to clear up his own notion of Tom's character; he neither believed in his pride nor his inconstancy. So he twirled his hat, and stopped short; then he opened the door, as if he might want to make a bolt of it, and turned towards Tom.

"Beg pardon, Squire, but have ye ever a message for little Kate?"

Tom Meredith stared for a minute at the old man, and then said, with tears in his eyes,

" No, Nat, no; not to-day; I've no message."

" No," said Tom Meredith to himself,
" I wish I could send Kate a message. I
wish I could tell her what a scoundrel she's
taking up with, and though I daresay I'm
no better than thousands of my fellow-creatures, I'm an honest man at all events, and
was a sober and happy one till she made me
otherwise."

This he said to himself, while Nat stood
in the doorway, hat in hand, looking somewhat reproachfully at his old friend and new
master.

Tom was right; he was an honest, good,
fellow, steady and persevering, and his esti-
mate of himself was a modest one. But
he was a little bit reckless, and the old
blood of the Merediths was stirring in him.
If Kate loved a gambler and a roysterer, he

was very likely to exhibit himself in very amiable colours before long.

Old Nat Gosling left the Squire also muttering to himself, for though he could not give vent to his pent-up wrath in the presence of Tom Meredith, he found it absolutely necessary to let some of it off before he was well out of the room. What he really did say just reached the ears of the Squire, and gave him something to think about as he went up to town by the mid-day mail.

"She's not just what she seems to be."

"No; she's not just what she seems to be, nor what she was two or three months ago," said Tom to himself; "more's the pity for us both." With which he mounted his phaeton, and hit the off horse so sharply as to upset his temper for the rest of the day. There are states of being in which one must hit something, and one of the surest signs of the old Adam in us is the sense of relief we feel when others suffer as well as we.

So Tom started for London.

"Good morning, Nat," said Mr. Joshua Masterman, just coming out of the stable yard as Nat Gosling came up. "I've been looking for you. There's Robert tells me that there's been somebody lurking about here all the morning, and he thinks he's after no good."

This was a few days later than the scene just recorded.

"Aye, aye, Mister Masterman; very like. Master Robert hisself isn't much good; what with beer and that precious appetite of his, he's putting on flesh every day, and he'll have to retire into private life now afore he's won a Derby. He's out o' all the two-year-old stakes already, and has nought but t' Coop to fall back upon."

Just then Robert appeared, and his personal appearance did not belie Nat Gosling's description. At this moment, too, Bob was bigger than usual with the news which he was carrying about with him.

"I say, Nat, I wanted you a while ago. Do you remember a friend o' Captain Goodge's—him as come round the paddocks one mornin', a fat old buffer, looked like a Jew, and called hisself Moses?"

"Yes, Bob. Money-lending old blackguard, I should think, by the look on him. What about him?" said Nat, confronting the too-stout boy, and looking mysterious.

"Why, nothin' perticular; but I see him here this mornin'."

"What time?"

Nothing Nat loved like a little cross-examination.

" Why, soon as it wor light ; just before the young 'uns went out."

" That shows as you worn't in bed as usual, Bob. And what was he doin'?"

" He wasn't doing anything perticler, but I thought you'd like to know. You see, Nat, Mr. Masterman didn't know the lot, so it worn't much use telling him."

Nat felt the compliment paid to his experience, though it seems Bob hadn't been able to keep it entirely to himself.

" No, no ; in course not. I'll take care o' that gentleman. I thought 1 know'd where them shifty tricks come from. They've been giving pepper to our horse at the corner. If I catch one of 'em about here, I'll give him pepper as he won't forget in a hurry. Mr. Masterman, which o' them boys belongs to Flying Scud?"

"Young Tom Piggott looks after him. He's in No. 14 now."

"Ah! I know him. He ain't a bad sort o' boy, but his father's a Methody—regular psalm-singer, and if you get one o' them Dissenters and a Jew together, dang'd if they wouldn't cheat the devil himself."

By which announcement you may conclude that old Nat was not too liberal in his religious opinions.

"And who is it, Nat? 'cos somebody's pulling the strings," said the boy.

"Well; I can't rightly say. In course, there's a gentleman at the bottom of it all. It ain't everybody as is like our Squire. Ah, if all the world was to go to work like him, there'd soon be no racing at all."

" Why so, Nat? I don't see why racing and honesty shouldn't go together."

"Because you're a booby. It ain't the racing, it's the robbery as they likes."

CHAPTER XVI.

NAT GOSLING AT HOME.

AFTER this, Nat Gosling went his rounds.
The old man's was an easy life of it; but,
when occasion demanded his services, he
could be brisk enough. For some reason
or other, just now, he began to be remarkably active about the stables. Whether he
thought that the Squire was likely to be
ruined, or whether he doubted the new
trainer's honesty or capacity, is not easy to
say. Nat had become an undoubted
authority among the boys; he even led a

gallop to their delight—which he did to perfection, notwithstanding his age; and he made his literary acquirements available, by giving the lads a Sunday evening lecture, theological as well as moral.

His honesty of purpose and industry fitted him for the latter; the former post might have been better filled by the curate of Middlethorpe, only they wouldn't have paid attention to him. The Bishop of Oxford, too, might have reasonably demurred to his definition of scriptural terms, of which the reader may be glad of an example.

"Now, Nat," said a persevering young proselyte, anxious for information; "you said you'd tell us what a Pharisee was."

Nat hummed and hawed for a long time, but he was sorely pressed by his juvenile auditors.

"Now, Nat, you know it is of no use if you don't explain," said Robert.

"Well, boys, you know — a Pharisee? why, you all know what a Pharisee is."

"No we don't, Nat; never heard tell on him afore."

"Quite sure?" said Nat.

"Quite sure," said the boys.

"Well, then," replied he, full of courage from their ignorance, not from his own, "he's a little white thing like a rabbut."

Such was Nat Gosling, in his office of jack-of-all-trades; and having looked well over the yearlings after exercise, and taken a last look at Flying Scud—having previously done the pigs, the few Southdowns that the Squire kept for his own eating, and the shorthorns which had been trans-

planted from Burleigh and Fawsley —
and having finally given a general lecture
on temperance and industry in the saddle-
room, over a pipe, he betook himself to his
home.

His home was not untenanted, though
Kate Rideout was absent. The chair of
honour, if it might so be called, was
occupied by one Mrs. Kettle. A warm-
hearted, good sort of woman she was, with
sharp black eyes, a great circumference of
visage, and figure too for that matter, and a
pagoda on the top of her head, which she
called a cap, covered with bows—rainbows
they might have been denominated from
the variety of their colours.

The late Kettle had died early in life of
a consumption of spirits and water, and the
disconsolate widow had sought refuge in
the housekeeper's room of the late John

Sykes. She was said to have had designs on the master, which failed; and she then transferred her attentions to Nat Gosling, whom she thought of making the second Mr. Kettle. Nat Gosling, however, in his widowhood was impervious to the tender passion. He was glad, notwithstanding, to see Mrs. Kettle, in the absence of Kate, and welcomed her graciously.

They conversed on divers subjects, of which the Squire and his prospects was one. Kate was gone to Mrs. Kirby, of Longgate, to spend the evening, and there was no necessity for reticence. Mrs. Kettle made tea, and added, as she said, for cholic, something that never came out of the pump.

"Ah! he's terribly changed, is Master Tom," said Nat. "This fortin of his has upset the coach ; he's noways in form, Mrs. Kettle."

" I don't mainly think it's the fortin, Master Gosling. You may depend on it there's a woman at the bottom of it. He goes to York, and he loses his money, and dines at the club, and stays away at this house and that. I don't think he's slept at home three nights out of the seven since the old man's death."

" That's a bad sign," said Nat, thoughtfully. " Ah ! it's the women, I expect."

" Oh ! and the men too—drat the men ;" for Mrs. Kettle didn't allow everybody the privilege of abusing her sex. " It ain't the women as wins his money; and I'm sure he can't get a better dinner at the York Club itself, though they do say great things of it, than I can put before him any day."

Mrs. Kettle then spread her rather coarse but very clean pocket-handkerchief over her knees, and proceeded to mingle buttered toast with her intelligence.

Nat Gosling was anxious to learn what he could of the squire's movements; and as he knew quite enough of domestic life to be certain that the housekeeper's room or the servant's hall got the first information, he asked, with a great appearance of simplicity, whether there was any "particular party as the master seemed to take to. None o' the Miss Quails, think ye, Mrs. Kettle?"

"Lor' bless you, Mr. Gosling. What! for the likes o' them to——"

"Nor Colonel Maynard's, nor Miss Silvertop, the great heiress? And yet you think there's a woman at the bottom of it all."

Here Nat turned the whole contents of his cup into his saucer, and drank it at a draught.

"Mr. Gosling, do you ever guess what's the matter wi' master? When he was plain Tom Meredith, did he ever come down here of a evening?"

"O' course he did, to ask about the horses, as in duty bound; now he ain't no call to come here you know, Mrs. Kettle."

"Folks did say something about our Kate, Mr. Gosling, and I do say as whatever happens, an honest man don't go about with the wind. Money's money, and love's love; and they didn't ought to be mixed up together."

"They very seldom are, Mrs. Kettle," said Nat again, sententiously.

"I say, it would be a fine thing for Kate,

there's no denying it. It 'ud be a fine
thing for your granddaughter to be mistress
o' the hall, Nat Gosling. It's a different
thing from a trainer's cottage. Better is a
dinner of herbs where love is than a round
of beef and hatred therewith."

Mrs. Kettle knew what she meant, but
her tea had been stronger than usual that
evening. However, the round of beef was
quite near enough.

"Do you know, Mrs. Kettle," said Nat,
looking through a cloud of tobacco-smoke
at the energetic widow, "do you know who
Kate is?"

"Kate's a great favourite of mine, Mr.
Gosling; but she's your granddaughter,
and it 'ud be a fine thing to be mistress of
Nobbley Hall."

"Kate Rideout isn't my granddaughter;
and if she was mistress of Nobbley Hall it

wouldn't be more than she deserves.
When old John Sykes was a dying he made
me promise to keep the secret till Kate was
of age. To-day is her twenty-first birthday, and I'll tell you all about it." Here
Nat Gosling lit a pipe, and continued his
story at solemn intervals between the puffs
of smoke. "Asking your pardon, Mrs.
Kettle, now we're on the subject, Kate
Rideout's mother was a distant relation of
your late master, John Sykes. She ran
away with a young officer from the farm-
house in which she was at service as a
dairymaid."

"Shameful hussy!" exclaimed Mrs.
Kettle.

"Wait a bit, marm," said Nat. "When
they went after her they found she was
married all right and regular, like an honest
woman. And as the young man had acted

like an honest man by her, his family refused to see her or him, and cut off the supplies. That's the reg'lar course, I'm told, when a gentleman behaves to a poor girl as he ought. I think I should be inclined to leave him a shilling or two, but they didn't. So they goes to India; and he gets killed, and dies; and she follows him; and all the property they sends back was this one poor little Kate. John Sykes educates her, and pervides for her, and they calls her my niece—or granddaughter, or something—'cos he knowed how charitable the world was, and what they'd ha' said of him for pervidin' for a poor relation. So, as I told t' Squire, she's not just what she seems."

Nat had got as far as this in his explanation of Kate's previous history, and Mrs. Kettle was enjoying it open-mouthed, when the door of the cottage was burst open, and Kate herself, as pale as a ghost, rushed into the room.

Her fright amounted to very little, after all. She had seen the notorious poacher, Mark Heron, in company with a most formidable-looking old Jew. It was moonlight, and she thought she recognized the stranger who had slept at Old Nat's cottage for a night or two previous to the funeral. She had not been accosted by them; nor did they appear to have been guilty of any very suspicious conduct. But she had heard them mention the name of Tom Meredith, coupled with some vague threats of vengeance; and Kate, usually courageous enough, conjured up terrors that at another time would scarcely have occurred to her as worth notice.

And when Kate had finished, she had to

listen to Nat Gosling's confession, to which he added some reminders, that Kate was now a lady of some fortune, and might aspire to the hand of something or somebody exceptional—even to a winner of the Derby; decidedly, in Nat's opinion, the man of the year.

It might reasonably have been expected that this revelation should have elated Kate Rideout; and in one respect it did. Her respectability of parentage, on her father's side, seemed to bridge over a sort of gulf between her and the Squire of Nobbley Hall. On any other score she was the Kate of old. Parents are valuable, and she regarded them in this light, as genitorial, pecuniary, protective, and educational aids.

These last three positions had been eminently forfeited by Captain and Mrs.

Rideout, who had brought her into the world, and had allowed her to shift for herself when in it.

"I don't know anything, Nat, about your being my grandfather or not," said the girl, when told of her genealogical claims on the late owner of Nobbley; "but I know that I have to thank you and John Sykes for everything in the world that I have, and I don't want to forget it. I should have been very happy to have remained your granddaughter, and I only hope you'll do your duty by that Mark Heron and the old Jew I've just met as you've done it by me."

"They're only after t' Scud, my girl; but I think we shall be too many for 'em yet;" with which he relapsed into a contemplation of Mrs. Kettle's head-dress.

Before that lady's retirement, however,

Nat Gosling produced some of old Mr. Sykes's very best port and sherry, and he and Mrs. Kettle proceeded to drink Kate's twenty-first birthday, and to wish her many years to enjoy the little bit of property that John Sykes had given her, at odd times, to say nothing of the legacy.

CHAPTER XVII.

WHILE matters were thus progressing at Nobbley and Middlethorpe, the *dramatis personæ* were not idle in London. Tom Meredith had reached his destination, and found himself at once in the buoyant waters of successful London life. The Squire's reputation had long preceded him. Old friends of his uncle, the Colonel, were willing to welcome him; and had sons—ill-natured people would have added daughters—who were not likely to remember anything to the disadvantage of so eligible a companion.

To tell the truth, there was very little to recollect; for it is a remarkable trait of good society that a man may be as poor as he pleases, without any interference on its part, and may "come again," as we say of a beaten horse, without any intrusive inquiries, so long as he comes with plenty to satisfy all demands, which, under those circumstances, are apt to be exigeant. Who in the world had troubled themselves about the Merediths when out of it? Who wanted to know whether what Grindley Goodge said of the antecedents of Tom Meredith was true or false? He was no great authority, and disappointed heirs were known to be spiteful. In fact, the report which he spread, or endeavoured to spread, among the men at Tattersall's, and at the clubs, was received with about the same favour as " I don't know whether you know it or not, but your horse has lost a fore-shoe," is received in the middle of a good run. "Which is it?" "The near foot," replies the obsequious stranger. "Ah! thanks: I dare say it won't hurt." *Sotto voce:* "Confound his stupidity! why couldn't he mind his own business? I dare say I should never have found it out till the run was over, and now I shall be fancying he goes lame at every stride."

What could it signify to old Lord Cruis-keen if Tom Meredith had been a bailiff, or a tenant farmer, or a trainer; he looked like a gentleman; the Merediths were very good people, heraldically considered; Tom rode and drove capital cattle, and gave good dinners, and played high, and lost his mo-ney like "one of us." Glenlivat was quite right to put him up at the Turf, and I shall go down and canvass for him. With the youngsters his family misfortunes created a strong sympathy, now that they had come right again; and it was quite a feather in his cap that the Colonel had ruined himself with gambling and extravagance, and left Tom to bear the brunt of it, and go into slavery for his uncle's debts. I don't know that one thrives so well on family ruin, unless one has a good Phœnix-like chance of coming out of the ashes all right again after a time.

One thing was quite clear: Tom was living as if he were determined to make up for lost time. His first appearance at the Corner (for it was the Corner, you know, in those days) put the Flying Scud in his right place, and Captain Goodge and Major Mulligan in the wrong one. As, however, those gentlemen and their friends had their own reasons for believing that the owner was either ignorant or dishonest, and that the Criterion winner was only intended for milking purposes, they felt no compunction in laying the odds pretty freely, as the price day after day became shorter, and takers more numerous. Tom Meredith made no mystery of his own opinion, and being one of those ill-mannered fools who speak the truth whenever they do open their mouths, he persuaded his friends that he had a colt as likely to win the Derby as any public horse in the betting, so they backed him accordingly.

Honesty is the best policy on the turf; for as few speak the truth or believe it, it is well calculated to deceive universally. Diplomacy is said to share its reputation and its defence.

If all that was said of Tom Meredith had been true, he need have won a fortune on the Derby, if his health lasted as long. I am not going to defend the system by which he was endeavouring to cheat himself into happiness or forgetfulness. It would be preferable, and more in accordance with some parts of his character, that he should have endeavoured to bear what his disordered imagination taught him to believe, or that he should have gone straightway, analytically or personally, into an investigation, which would have been attended with very little inconvenience, and certain relief to himself and Kate Rideout.

However, Tom's present position is one of an entirely exceptional kind. The conviction that we have been deceived where we had the greatest reason to trust, is, of all things, the hardest to bear—the most agonizing, the most distracting ; and to talk of inconsistency in such a crisis is only to describe the natural result of the trial upon a strong and nervous mind; so Tom wallowed in all the extravagance of sensual pleasure, and made his body a slave to fifty passions, while his mind was the slave but of one.

And while the Squire—much abused name in the days we live in!—was wasting his substance in riotous living, another of our acquaintances by no means confined his attention to his betting-book and its accompaniments. Grindley Goodge had other irons in the fire. To say that Grindley Goodge, or any rascal of the same kind, was in love in its best sense, is to give them credit for more than they are capable of. From the moment he had set eyes on Kate

Rideout he had conceived a violent and misdirected passion for the girl; and the circumstance of her unprotected situation, as one of his own tenants (as far as he could understand), gave him hopes which his knowledge of her character would not have excited.

Unfortunately her own request to him, made in behalf of Tom Meredith, and a coquettish manner, natural to her, and increased by her position as a suppliant to him, encouraged those hopes. It was not a time for Kate to have resented, severely, any impertinent allusions, or presumptive gallantries, as long as they were confined to words, nor did she do so. She was quite willing to trust to her own resources at any future time to relieve herself from the results of that interview, in which she begged and received a favour. Grindley Goodge, too, whose very passion was tinged with avarice and revenge, attached double importance to the pursuit of his object, by reflecting that Nat Gosling and Flying Scud might be assailable through Kate ; and that Tom Meredith's punishment would be doubly severe if it deprived him of a Derby and a mistress at the same time. Any idea of the honourable love that Tom felt for the girl herself, after his restoration to his true position, was inconceivable to Goodge.

The cloth was still on the breakfast-table at Captain Goodge's lodgings in Piccadilly. The confederates were together, and discussing the chances of Rasper for the Two Thousand, which was to be run in a fortnight's time.

"After that the Derby will be unpleasantly close for some of us. However, I presume the trial was quite right," said Goodge, helping himself to a cigar.

" Quite right, as far as we can possibly ascertain. I own the manner in which the horse has been backed since Meredith's arrival in town would have staggered me but for Mark Heron's assurance," said Major Mulligan.

" And what does that amount to ?" inquired Chouser.

" That he was close by at the time ; that the boys both say it was right. He examined them separately, and one is a relation of his own ; and that he knows Nat Gosling would like to do Meredith a turn for the way he treated some girl at the farm ; and that's the reason he's let him back the horse as he has done."

" Two strings to one's bow, Mulligan, is

an Englishman's motto, and we've got too
much money on it to run any risk. What
with Woodbie, and Fitzwalter, and the
money we've got out of Meredith, who's as
green as grass, we can go on for a bit;
but if the Derby comes off wrong, I must
go."

So spake Grindley Goodge, in a manner which had nothing but earnestness
about it.

"And I shall retire upon me friend Davis.
Faith, I'll be mortgaging me interest in
Castle Mulligan, and I'll look to Mo. there
to help me out of the scrape," said Major
Mulligan.

"S'help me, I shall be in the 'ole myself,"
said the Jew. "There's Captain Goodge's
thousand, and Mr. Chouser's seven hundred, and Lord Woodbie's bill for two thousand——"

"Why, hang it, Mo., what an old Jew you are; you know he only got thirteen hundred for it."

"And a fine Rembrandt, you remember—a very fine Rembrandt—worth six hundred, at least."

"A copy; for which Christy offered him forty-two pounds. Besides, he's as safe as the church," said Chouser.

"Vich, Mr. Chouser, yours or mine? Ah! it ain't just vot it vas. There's guardians and fathers, and all sorts of natural obstacles to gentlemen spending of their money. And they plead their minority—and Lord Woodbie isn't of age. Oh! we must win, or I'll be in the 'ole." So sighed Mo. Davis.

"We must win," said Goodge, who, at all events, was a man of action. "We must win. Now, Davis, we shall make it all safe, if you'll do as I tell you. The first thing you'll do will be to go down to the north. I'd go myself, but they know me too well. You'll get hold of my friend, Mark Heron—you know whereabouts to find him; and as you're a client of old Quail, there won't be much difficulty about that. You must go to work with Mark; he's safe enough. He owes Meredith a grudge, which he'll pay with interest. He had him in once for three months, and he hasn't forgotten it. The first thing is the boys. One's enough—the boy that takes care of the Scud. It's young Tom Piggott. He's come of a bad lot—they're all Dissenters. It's no use to heat too many irons, if you want but one. See what's to be done with the boy first."

"They're such liars, are them boys, Captain; they'd take your spondoolics, and then sell ye to the other party. I don't like boys."

"No fear with an old file like you, Mo. I should like to see the boy that would get anything out of you for nothing. However, the thing must be done, and as we must stay here, I wish you would go down to Nobbley. It's too delicate a business to trust to everybody. If you report well, I'll run down myself; and I would now that Meredith's away, but I'd rather not be seen till a little later. Have you done anything for Meredith yet? He must have spent a year's income in the last month."

"Not yet. His paper's valuable at present, and there's some of it out in the City. They'll come to me by-and-bye."

"And if you'll come to me in the

17—2

evening, I'll tell you how to proceed at Nobbley."

Which he did, and the result of which we shall see hereafter.

CHAPTER XVIII.

"WHAT ARE THE ODDS AS LONG AS YOU'RE HAPPY."

WE must return now for a while to Lord Woodbie. He was a delightful type of the utterly reckless young English gentleman. He was, up to the code of honour established for general guidance in fashionable society, a perfect gentleman. There was a coolness, a perfect *sang froid*, in all his proceedings, in contemplating which it seemed marvellous that he should be ruining himself so rapidly. He had always had a taste for fast life of the high school, in which, in an inverse ratio to the apparent absence of all effort, was the effect wrought.

And we live, happily, in days when a man is so far independent of convention that he may make a beggar and an exile of himself in any way that he pleases, so long as he reaches that consummation at last. Lord Woodbie knew that there were many roads leading to the devil, and at first he was under some difficulty as to choice. He hung a long time between the Mecænas-like occupation of theatrical patronage with a prima donna, and the popular character of an Apicius. The first he rejected from a sense of its servility ; the latter from its utter inadequacy to the end proposed. The prevailing taste of the day led him to New-market and the Shires.

While yet an undergraduate he had a

string at the headquarters of turf business, and was in treaty for the Poundingshire hounds, as soon as the present master had finished his occupation. It was supposed that another year would about do for him. He had had then four (and no one ever exceeds five) seasons in a fashionable county.

The room in which we now find him was moderately sized, and most exquisitely furnished. On the left of the door, upon entering, was a long table, round which stood some twelve or fourteen men, all of them dressed as gentlemen who have lately left the table, but exhibiting in their demeanour and appearance a wide variety of intellectual and genealogical type. They stood round while the caster, shaking the dice-box, called his main, and backed it.

In the centre was a table, not unlike the table d'hôte of the Hotel des Princes or the Grand in Paris, where plate-glass, flowers, fruit, and champagne and claret invited the players to refresh themselves after a successful *coup*. There is nothing so appetising as winning a thousand or two.

On the right of the room was another table, more frequented, perhaps, than the hazard-table. It was covered with a roulette cloth, and the ball continued to roll while the players were invited to make their game.

Here and there, between the two, or standing over the fireplace discussing the chances of the Two Thousand candidates, were small knots of men, with their pencils and betting-books in hand.

"Will nobody back anything," said a languid voice from the centre.

" Yes, I will — seven. Seven it is —
wait till I've thrown out. Don't go, old
fellow. Seven—five. I'll take the odds.
I'll tell you what I'll do. I'll lay you four
hundred—five it is; that's seven monkeys
you owe me, Cardington. I'll lay you four
hundred to one against the Scud for the
Derby, if you'll lay me five to two against
Rasper for the Guineas. Come, that's on
the square."

" No, I can't back the Scud at that price.
You want Meredith——"

At that moment the door swung open,
and Tom Meredith walked into the
room.

" What's that, Woodbie?" and he pulled
out his book. " I'll take you four hundred
to one—again, if you like."

" Write it down, Meredith." Which he
did.

Tom Meredith had been drinking; he was perfectly master of himself, but there was an excited look about him, and his eyes were restless and inflamed. His face, too, had become thinner, even in these few weeks, though he was still as handsome as ever, and an excellent type of the English country gentleman. There was no man who showed birth more palpably, in spite of every disadvantage, than Tom Meredith. There was, however, a weary look about him, and a worn expression of face, which seldom lighted up, excepting on the subject of his Derby colt.

Among the players at either table were the Duke of Cadwallo, Lord Glenlivat, Fitzwarren, Colonel Cardington, Goodge, and Mulligan. They made way for Meredith, who took the box and threw out at once. As he looked up, he saw Goodge and Mulligan, and returned the formal bow of the first by equally slight and formal recognition; with Major Mulligan he was less particular; and had the bowing and betting acquaintance of every-day life. His position with Grindley Goodge, after what had occurred, was peculiar. He would willingly have ignored him, had it been possible, but it was not.

At men's rooms, at the club, at Tattersall's, everywhere he met with him; and from the first moment he had been betrayed into a sort of recognition of him. A decided quarrel would have jeopardised the reputation of Kate; better let things take their chance, and avoid familiarity with one whom he had reason to regard as a scoundrel and his enemy.

After playing, with very bad luck, for half-an-hour, he turned to leave the clubhouse, and was greeted by Lord Woodbie, with whom he had become tolerably intimate.

"Come home with me, Meredith; it's hot, and I'm tired of this; come and have a rubber, or a game at écarté."

Meredith assented, and they walked slowly down to Grosvenor-square.

"Put lights in the small library, and lay out the card-tables; and put some supper and champagne into the dining-room. Has anybody been here?"

No one had been there. At that moment there was a knock at the door.

"Sir Felix Graham and Mr. Fitzwarren," and the servant shut the door.

"What did you do, Graham?"

"I lost a thou; and Fitz won three hundred of it. I'm come here to get it back again."

This ingenious confession inspired no anxiety, as Graham was proverbially unlucky.

"Then let us begin, or you'll have a participator in your success. I believe Mulligan and Chouser are coming."

"Who's the woman I saw with the Major in the phaeton? They say she's a daughter or a niece."

"Something of the sort; a niece, I believe," said Woodbie, who felt obliged to say something; and he blushed as he said it.

"They say Glenlivat's a good deal there. Old Cruiskeen won't like that."

"The girl would have the worst of it, I should think. Latimer is quite as good a man as Glenlivat; and I know no harm of Major Mulligan, or his family."

Lord Woodbie spoke rather more argumentatively than the subject seemed to require.

"All I mean to say is, that as Glen has no money, and Mulligan can't be a millionaire, the match wouldn't be to old Cruiskeen's liking. She'd look well enough as a countess, whenever the old boy goes; but beauty won't pay the mortgages on the Glenlivat property, Woodbie."

"But you think she would look well as a countess, Felix."

"She's the best looking woman I've seen, and I intend to cultivate the Major."

Here there came another knock at the door.

"Then you've nothing to do but to drop another thou to night, and let part of it go into his pocket," observed Fitzwarren, languidly.

" What does he give you at billiards, Woodbie?"

" Nothing. I can give him ten out of a hundred. He plays rather a flukey game, or I think I could manage fifteen."

Fitzwarren thought not, so did Meredith; but it was no use to say so; so the young nobleman continued happy in his delusion.

The Major arrived, and with him, not Chouser, but Goodge. Then the party agreed to a pool at écarté, which they played till four in the morning, the principal winners being Meredith and Sir Felix Graham; but there was no great mischief done, and revenge was promised at the Major's house at no distant period.

Somebody says that revenge is sweet. I hope these gentlemen found it so. But I have my doubts of the truth of that proverb, when it costs six or seven hundred pounds. You may give too much money for a sovereign.

This was precisely the case three nights afterwards, when Major Mulligan entertained a select party at his own house, the only individual of the party utterly indifferent to losses or gains being Lord Woodbie. That gentleman had been exceedingly piqued, without certifying it to himself by the association of any name but his own with Julia Latimer; and as Lord Glenlivat was just the sort of person to be emulated rather than followed, Lord Woodbie determined to ascertain before long the exact position he held in the lady's estimation. In fact, he was very seriously in love, and, although Lady Woodbie and Lord Cruiskeen, and plenty more earls and countesses, might have turned up their noses at the *mesalliance*, good luck or Providence. had brought his juvenile lordship face to face with a very worthy object for the exercise of his affection. So he lost and won, and lost again, cheered by the presence of his divinity, who presided in her uncle's drawing-room, until the lateness of the hour and the heaviness of the stake, warned her that it was time to retire.

Lord Glenlivat had the best of the play and the worst of the game, and was easily consoled for the preference given to Lord Woodbie by getting back some of his lost thousand.

Woodbie had quite ignored the pleasures of écarté, where the lucky abundance of kings in his adversary's hands accounted for his losses, until he had handed over all his ready money, and was wondering where he was to find a few hundreds more for to-morrow. The dilemma was solved by a most respectable old gentleman with a curious accent, who had watched the various encounters with considerable interest, but who had declined playing.

"I O U's," said he, upon seeing one of them across the table, " is nothing. Give a little bill, that's my way : you owe seven hundred, Lord Woodbie." Then and there, to the apparent astonishment of the party, he drew forth a large pocket book, full of acceptances and bills of all sorts. "There, get upon the back of that : just put your name across there. It's for von thousand at three months' interest, at ten per shent; no commission charged; no nothin'—just as a friend : that's von hundred more. Now, Major Mulligan, you give Lord Woodbie two hundred change. There, now you got your money. His lordship's got somethin' in hand, and then he'll pay me the thousand pounds ven he can. We always renews."

"I don't see the great advantage," said Lord Woodbie, laughing, and pocketing the notes.

"Vy, you're all satisfied, and it makes the time pass so quick. The three months 'll go like winking, ven you're on the back of a good bill."

END OF VOL. I.

BILLING, PRINTER, GUILDFORD.

www.ingramcontent.com/pod-product-compliance
Lightning Source LLC
Chambersburg PA
CBHW031347070726
47496CB00017B/1811